Spencer Hill Press

First Edition: March 2013.

Darby Karchut
Finn Finnegan : a novel / by Darby Karchut – 1st ed.
p. cm.
Summary:
A modern-day 13-year-old boy battles goblins in his suburban neighborhood with the help of a mythical knight.

The author acknowledges the copyrighted or trademarked status and trademark owners of the following wordmarks mentioned in this fiction: Wal-Mart, Jeep, Lord of the Rings, The Farmer's Almanac, Louisville Slugger

"Fire in the Head" lyrics by Arthur Hinds used with the permission of Arthur Hinds and Emerald Rose.

Cover design by K. Kaynak
Interior layout by Marie Romero

ISBN 978-1-937053-32-1 (paperback)
ISBN 978-1-937053-33-8 (e-book)

Printed in the United States of America

Finn Finnegan

Book One
of
The Adventures of
Finn MacCullen

Darby Karchut

SPENCER HILL PRESS

Dedicated to the memory of Lloyd Alexander
1924 - 2007

(Well, well, what do you know? A bard, after all.)

Also by Darby Karchut

Gideon's Spear
(Spencer Hill Press—February 2014)

Griffin Rising
(Twilight Times Books)
Griffin's Fire
(Twilight Times Books)
Griffin's Storm
(Copper Square Studios—December 2012)

Non-fiction
Money and Teens: Savvy Money Skills
(Copper Square Studios)

The Song of the Tuatha De Danaan

I am a wind on the sea,
I am a wave of the ocean,
I am the roar of the sea,
I am a bull of seven battles,
I am a hawk on the cliff,
I am a teardrop of sunlight,
I am a gentle herb,
I am a boar enraged,
I am a salmon in a pool,
I am a lake in a plain,
I am the vigor of man
I am the meaning of poetry,
I am a spear on the attack, pouring forth combat,
I am the god who fires your mind.

Pronunciation of Words and Phrases

Tuatha De Danaan (tua day dhanna): An ancient warrior race of mythical beings from Ireland

Amandán (AH-mon-dan): Goblin-like creatures

Fáilte (FALL-sha): *Welcome*

Céad mile fáilte (kad MEEL-a FALL-sha): *A hundred thousand welcomes*

Gle mhaith (glay moth): *Very good*

Codladh sumh (CUL-la sovh): *Sleep well*

Poc sídhe (poke she): *Fey, or fairy, stroke*

Slainte (SLAWN-che): *Health*

Faugh a ballagh (FOW-an BALL-ah): *Clear the Way!*

One

"Son of a goat!" The boy swore and jumped back. A second squirt of bird poop landed with a plop, this time on the toe of his shoe. "Oh, real funny," he said with a grimace. He glared up at the crow swinging back and forth on the power line overhead, sooty wings spread wide for balance. The bird cocked its head and stared back, its eye a red-rimmed marble.

"Are you trying to warn me?" The boy dragged the tip of his sneaker through the lawn bordering the sidewalk. He wrinkled his nose at the stink of wet bird droppings mingled with the aroma of freshly mowed grass. Not a good combination. "Or are you just yanking me around?" He watched as the crow crouched for a moment as if deciding, then hoisted itself into the air and flew off. The boy snorted. "Yup, just what I thought—yanking."

Slipping his arms free from the straps of a half-full backpack, he dropped it to the ground as he fanned his worn tee shirt, trying to dry the patch of sweat between his shoulder blades. Pushing a mop of auburn hair out of his eyes, he frowned, scanning the peaceful neighborhood. *Aw, this is crazy,* he thought. *I'm never going to find him.*

And even if I do, what if he says no? Then what? I can't go back home. Not now.

Picking up his pack, he slung it over one shoulder and continued down the street. He studied every house, each one exhibiting pride of ownership with a well-tended yard. *Somehow, I can't imagine him living in one of* those. He slowed, then stopped when he reached the end of the cul-de-sac.

A small house sat by itself next to an empty lot. Old-fashioned in a cottage-y way, it was painted the same shade of rusty green as the pine trees flanking either end of its broad porch. Wooded foothills rose behind it, while proud mountains strutted away further west. A massive stone wall, as high as his chin, bordered the yard.

Shifting from foot to foot, he peered at the wrought-iron gate bisecting the wall. His heart sped up when he noticed a Celtic knot gracing the center of the gate. Beyond, a flagstone walkway snaked through the shaggy lawn. Stretching the length of the northern wall, a thick hedge bristled with broad, saw-toothed leaves and spiny stalks. A few spots along the hedge were plucked bald. On the other side of the hedged wall, a battered pickup truck, gray with age, rested in the graveled driveway.

Relief flooded the boy at the sight of the deadnettle hedge. *This has gotta be the right house.* He was reaching for the latch when the screen door creaked opened. He froze.

"Now, just where would ye be going?" asked a deep voice. A man stepped out and sauntered to the edge of the porch. A head above average height with a whipcord build, he wore a faded denim shirt, open over a white tee shirt. Hooking his thumbs into his jeans pockets, he rested a shoulder against one of the wooden columns, curiosity on his lean face.

"I'm-I'm looking for someone. I know he lives on this street, but I can't remember his address."

Before he could say more, a shadow ghosted across the yard. Man and boy stiffened and looked up. A crow soared overhead, a black X wheeling in a tight circle against the sun. It cawed sharply, just once, and glided away.

The boy whirled to face the street, his heart slamming against his ribs and the pack slipping from his shoulder. His eyes darted from shadow to shadow, looking for any sign of movement. A sharp whistle pulled his head around.

The man stood at the bottom of the steps, a knife the length of his forearm in one hand. The blade was a bronze flame. "Come, boyo," he said, his voice low and urgent. "Get behind me on the porch. Quickly, now, before they attack."

The boy hesitated, glancing at the knife, and then shoved the gate open with a clang. He winced when it bounced off the wall, swung back, and smacked his elbow. Cursing under his breath, he ran across the yard and darted around the man, taking the steps two at a time. Grabbing a broom propped next to the door, he tucked the bristled end under one arm, gripping his makeshift weapon like a jousting lance. Armed, he licked his lips and took a position behind the man on the edge of the porch.

"Have ye a blade?" the man asked over his shoulder as he scanned the neighborhood.

"Does it look like I have one?"

"A bit cheeky." The man glanced back. "For someone wielding a broom."

"I'd have taken a pitchfork, but, hey, this was all you had."

The man raised an eyebrow. "Make that *very* cheeky." He continued to survey the area. The rumble of a garbage truck echoed from the next block over. An automatic sprinkler squirted on in the yard across the street.

After a few more minutes of vigilance, the man relaxed and turned around. Flipping the knife into the air with a practiced move, he caught it by the handle and tucked it into a sheath hanging from his belt under the tail of his denim shirt.

"Well, boyo, the manky bird may be playing us for fools. They do that from time to time instead of warning us about the Amandán," he said, his voice colored green with an Irish lilt. "Lesson number one. When I tell ye to move, I mean run like the very devil is behind ye. Those goblins are almost impossible to spot when camouflaged. And they're bleedin' fast. Very fast."

"Got it." The boy leaned the broom against the side of the house and wiped his sweaty hands on his jeans. A look of recognition spread across his face when he noticed the thick ring of twisted gold loosely encircling the man's neck. "Hey, you're him!"

"And just who might I be?"

"You're the Knight, Gideon Lir. I was looking for you. I'm …," he began.

"...Finnegan MacCullen," Gideon finished for him. "Me new apprentice. Who, for some unknown reason, has unexpectedly arrived on me doorstep a day early."

Two

"I go by Finn, not Finnegan." He inched closer to the edge of the porch.

"*Céad míle fáilte*," Gideon said with a nod. He raked strong fingers through his black hair, then pointed toward the gate. "Well, 'Finn not Finnegan'. Don't just stand there—fetch yer kit."

"Oh, yeah." Finn trotted down the steps and across the yard, aware of Gideon's gaze on him. He hurried to his pack. Taking advantage of having his back to the Knight, Finn pulled up his shirt and gave his face a swipe. Reaching with one hand for the pack, he tried to smooth his hair with the other hand.

"Close the gate behind ye," Gideon ordered and headed toward the house.

Finn jogged back, his pack swinging from one shoulder. He followed the Knight inside, swallowing. *So far, so good. At least he didn't tell me to come back tomorrow.*

"Leave yer bag for now." Gideon gestured toward a wooden crate next to the door. The box contained a pair of mud-caked work boots, several dirty rags, and a tin pail. A row of coat hooks above it held a canvas hunting jacket. As Finn dropped his pack, Gideon closed the door behind him. "Join me in the kitchen. We'll speak over an early lunch."

Finn looked around as he trailed the Knight across the main room, the last touch of the late morning sun skimming through a wide pair of windows. He eyed the shabby furniture cluttering the small room. A stone fireplace took up most of one wall. His face lit up at the assortment of knives, daggers, and a few hatchets, all of bronze, resting horizontally on pegs above the mantel. Books filled the shelves on the opposite side of the room, next to a battered but tidy desk tucked under the stairs leading up to the second floor.

Stepping into the kitchen in the rear of the house, Finn's stomach growled at the rich aroma of lamb and herbs and potatoes rising from the steaming pot on the stove. "That smells good." He sniffed. "What is it?"

"Why, Irish stew, of course." Gideon walked over to the stove, giving the pan a stir. "Hand me a couple of bowls. They're in the cupboard next to the sink."

Gideon ladled a generous portion in each one, passed them to Finn, then followed him over to the table in the corner of the room, carrying a still-warm loaf of brown bread wrapped in a clean cloth. Pulling out his chair, he motioned for Finn to take a seat across from him. Uncovering the loaf, he cut several thick slabs and handed one to Finn.

"Did you bake this?" Finn asked.

"I did."

"But-but you're a Knight."

"Aye, 'tis true. I am also a Knight who likes to eat." He raised his eyebrows in surprise when Finn began wolfing down stew between bites of bread. "And apparently, so do ye." He tasted a spoonful. "And how are yer aunt and uncle?"

"They're fine," Finn mumbled around a mouthful of food, both elbows propped on the table. He spat a chunk of turnip back into his bowl with a *plunk*.

Gideon grimaced, but said nothing. He gazed at the boy, his eyes the same uncanny shade of sky blue as Finn's. "'Tis odd that they would deliver ye a day early, without any warning or a by-yer-leave to me."

Finn shifted in his chair. "Um … I … Well, Uncle was driving down from Denver today, so I figured I'd save him an extra trip tomorrow." He hunched over the bowl and shoveled another spoonful into his mouth, eyes fixed on the table as he ate.

"Curious. I was reading in the front room with the windows open for the last hour and never heard a car pull up."

"He dropped me off at the corner. He was kind of in a hurry." Finn took another bite and swallowed it down half-chewed.

"In a hurry."

"Yeah."

Finn peeked up through his bangs as the Knight pushed his bowl aside and rested his elbows on the table, fingers steepled together. The *tick-ticking* of the cooling stove filled the kitchen as he waited.

And waited.

And waited.

Finn broke.

"Okay, he didn't actually bring me." He wiped his mouth on his arm. "I walked."

"Sorry?"

"I walked."

"From Denver? To High Springs?" Gideon dropped his hands, his mouth sagging open. "That's over sixty miles!"

"I got a ride most of the way. With some college students going home for the summer."

"Ye hitchhiked?"

"Yeah, I do it all the time. It's no big deal. They dropped me off downtown and I walked from there." He looked down and poked at the stew. "I didn't want to bother anyone, so—"

"Stop." Gideon held up a hand. "Ye gods," he muttered under his breath, then shoved his chair back with a screech and headed to

7

the counter. "Their number?" he asked, snatching the phone from its cradle.

"They're not home."

"I dinna ask ye where they were. I asked ye for their bleedin' phone number." He punched it in as Finn grudgingly recited it.

"Hullo, Owen. This is Gideon Lir. Fine, thank ye. Listen, the reason I'm calling is that Finnegan is here. In High Springs." He frowned. "Finnegan MacCullen." His frown deepened. "Yer nephew. Red hair, blue eyes, atrocious table manners." His eyes flicked once toward the boy scraping his bowl clean. "Aye, I'm still taking him. But ye might wish to know the stunt he pulled. I thought ye'd be worried about him, so I …" He paused and listened for several long minutes, his black brows pinching together. "And ye dinna think to inform me about his mother until *now?*" He turned his back and lowered his voice. "'Tis a bit under the table." Gideon pinched the bridge of his nose as he continued to listen. "Aye, well, it appears we're *both* ankle-deep in the situation," he said, clipping the words. "Right. I'll tell him." He hung up the phone.

Silence filled the kitchen. After a moment, Gideon spoke over his shoulder. "They weren't even aware ye had left this morning."

Finn shrugged. "Figures. I'm not exactly the favorite in the family."

"Because of yer mother's people?"

"I guess."

"They wished ye luck, if that helps."

"They try to be nice to me, but they're really busy. They've got nine kids. And my cousin, Liam, is starting *his* apprenticeship next month, so they're doing a bunch of stuff for his ceremony. That's why I decided to just get out of their way." He paused for a moment. "So-so I guess they told you about me."

"Aye, they did." Gideon turned around and leaned against the counter.

Raising his chin, Finn steeled himself. "Are you going to send me back?"

Gideon ran his knuckles along his jaw. He hesitated before speaking. "I'll give ye the truth of it. I wasn't expecting ..." His voice trailed off.

Finn glanced away. "Someone like me." The stew congealed in his stomach as his fists clenched under the table. He looked up when Gideon cleared his throat.

"So, tell me, Finnegan MacCullen. Yer mother—was she half or whole?"

"Half. My mom was half human."

Gideon sighed, then shook his head, his face unreadable. "Although I do not hold yer bloodline against ye, I should show ye the door this minute. The agreement with yer family to train ye was made under a false pretense."

Finn's heart twisted. He nodded numbly, trying to ignore the lump in his throat. *He's going to kick me out without even giving me a chance,* he thought. *Now what do I do?* He kept his eyes fixed in front of him as the Knight continued.

"And just why should I take ye on as my apprentice, eh?" He held up a hand and began ticking off on his fingers. "Ye're cheeky. Ye're woefully lacking in manners, except bad ones. And ye're part mortal. Ye've not much in yer favor, boyo. Can ye give me one good reason I should let ye stay?"

"No," Finn whispered.

"No? Well, I can." Gideon fingered the torc around his throat. "And so, ye shall stay."

Finn snapped his head around. Astonished, he opened and closed his mouth several times before he could speak. "W-why?"

"Because, me lad, ye were willing to go into battle by me side today. Armed with only a broom." The corner of the Knight's mouth quirked into a half smile. "Ye are, Finnegan MacCullen, no coward."

For a long minute, they gazed at one another. Outside the open kitchen window, a chickadee whistled its three-note song, calling its mate home.

Then, Gideon straightened. "Now, go fetch yer things. Then, I'll show ye yer room." He waited until the boy left the room before shaking his head. *Ye gods,* he thought. *I did not see this coming.* Staring blankly at Finn's place at the table, he ran a hand down his face. *And just how am I to train an apprentice who's part mortal?* Deep in thought, he began carrying the empty bowls to the sink. Halfway across the kitchen, a wicked smile spread across his face. *Of course, I'm forgetting one of the advantages of having an apprentice.* He dropped the dishes into the sink with a clatter, cast a contemptuous eye on the rest of the mess, and wiped his hands on his shirt.

The free labor.

Three

"Oh, wow, my own room," Finn breathed as he paused in the doorway. Stepping farther in, he tossed his pack on the narrow bed and walked around to the window. The wooden shutters screeched when he pushed them apart. He gazed out from his second-floor window at a spacious backyard bordered on three sides with the same stone wall as the front. In the middle of the yard stood two tall posts with a cable stretched tight between them. A lumpy burlap bag dangled from a rope attached to the cable; it hung over a patch of bare ground. Beyond the back wall, wooded acres stretched westward toward the foothills. Finn noticed a trail leading from the other side of wall into the woods.

"Yer own bath, too," Gideon said. He pointed with his chin toward the adjoining room. "And yer to keep both of them tidy."

"No problem." Finn reached over and started to unzip his backpack when Gideon cleared his throat. He looked up.

"As it appears yer apprenticeship has begun, albeit a day early, ye best start learning some rules."

"Like what?"

"Like the use of 'yes, sir' and 'no, sir' when ye address me. Ye may also call me Gideon." He paused, then added, "Or Knight Gideon if ye're trying to—what's the modern phrase—suck up to me?"

Finn's face warmed. Catching himself before he said something that would most likely be labeled as *cheeky*, he nodded. "Yes, sir."

"Right." Gideon nodded toward the pack. "Work away."

Fighting the temptation to snap off a salute, Finn grabbed the bag and shook it upside-down. Several balled-up tee shirts, a gray hoodie, and a pair of jeans tumbled out, followed by socks, underwear, a toothbrush, and one smooth stone.

"Yer father's, I take it?" Gideon stepped closer and picked up the pale rock, running a thumb over its creamy surface. He laid it in the palm of his hand to examine it. His skin showed dimly through its translucent edges.

"Yup." Finn stuffed the shirts and jeans into one of the drawers of the dresser standing in the corner. "I mean, yes, sir," he said over a shoulder. *Yes, sir. No, sir. How high, sir?* "Did you know my dad and mom?"

"I dinna. Although I heard Fergus MacCullen was one of the finest hunters of his time." Gideon placed the stone on the nightstand and sat down on the foot of the bed. He gestured toward the remaining objects scattered across the faded, but clean, comforter. "'Twas all ye brought?"

"It's all I got."

"Nine children, eh? Ye're fortunate to have yer own toothbrush."

Finn made a face. "Eww. Gross!" He scooped his up and headed to the bathroom.

Gideon called after him. "After ye're done here, we'll make plans about tomorrow morning. I'm assuming yer aunt and uncle won't be attending yer ceremony?"

Finn shrugged as he returned. "We could just skip it if you want. It's no big deal."

"Finnegan MacCullen, turning thirteen and becoming an apprentice is a *big deal*, as ye put it. Ye're following the ancient path of the Tuatha De Danaan, warriors who have fought the long fight against the Amandán for thousands of years." He tapped the gold torc around his neck for emphasis. "Do not minimize these first steps on yer journey."

"What's a *two-a-day dhanna?*"

Gideon's eyebrows shot up. "Why, 'tis the ancient Celtic name of our kind. The Fey. The Host of the Hills. The Fair Folk."

"Oh, yeah, I forgot. Uncle Owen usually just said *our people.*"

The Knight started to speak, then stopped and pointed to the wooden chair by the small desk. "Sit, boyo. We need to talk."

"About the ceremony?" Finn asked, tilting the chair and balancing back on two legs. He lowered the chair with a thump at Gideon's frown.

"No. About the falsehood ye gave when I first asked how ye got here. Dishonesty is something I'll not tolerate. We may have to bend the truth from time to time around mortals, but we do not lie to each other. Under any circumstances." His eyes bore into Finn's. "Do so again, Finnegan MacCullen, and ye'll find yerself suffering the consequences. Now, do we understand each other?"

Finn gulped. "Yes, sir."

With a curt nod, Gideon rose. "Finish unpacking, then downstairs with ye."

"Yes, sir." He waited until Gideon left, then walked over to the bed and flopped back on it. Every bone in his body sagged with exhaustion from sneaking out of his uncle's house before dawn, making his way to the highway on foot, then spending an hour on the shoulder working up the courage to stick out his thumb for a ride. He blew out a long breath.

I can't believe he's letting me stay, he thought, staring up at the ceiling. His eyes traced a crack in the plaster. *And that he didn't send me away because I'm a halfer.*

Rolling to his side, Finn gazed at the stone on the nightstand. He reached over and grabbed it, rattling it around in his cupped hand, its shape as familiar to him as his own face. *I can't wait to see it light up and show everyone that I'm De Danaan, too.* Clutching it in his fist, he pressed it against his chest. *I hope I remember all the words to the Song.* He squeezed his eyes shut and began chanting the first line.

And dozed off.

Two hours later, Finn jerked awake. Squinting, he looked around the unfamiliar room bathed in afternoon light. His glance fell on the clock next to the bed.

"Oh, no," he moaned. He rolled off the rumpled cover and shot out of the room. Running down the stairs, he stumbled when he missed the bottom step. Recovering, he flung himself into the living room. "Sorry about that," he panted. "I fell asleep."

"Apparently." Gideon closed his book with a snap and tossed it on the desk before him; his chair creaked as he sat back. "The next time I tell ye to do something, boyo, I expect instant obedience. It may save yer arse one day." Swiveling around, he pointed to a stool close by.

"Yes, sir." Finn sank down, his eyes wary. As he waited, he picked at a frayed hole in his jeans, aware of Gideon silently examining his worn clothing and too-long hair.

"Nervous, are ye?" the Knight asked after a long minute.

"Actually, I'm good." Finn plastered a fake grin on his face.

"Actually, ye're a bold liar. There ye sit, yer mind filled with the horror stories about us tyrannical Knights, and how we train our apprentices with long hours and brutal expectations. Am I right?"

"I don't know. Maybe."

Gideon leaned forward, their knees almost touching. "Well, the tales ye've been told are all true, Finnegan MacCullen." His hands shot out, capturing the boy's in a grip of iron.

Finn gasped. He wobbled on the stool, heart in his throat. The rough calluses on Gideon's fingers scraped against the inside of his wrists. He tried to pull away, but the Knight tightened his grip.

"Be warned, young De Danaan," Gideon said, his voice deepening as he spoke. "'Twill be years of misery ahead of ye. Ye'll train, day and night, heat and cold, until ye weep from exhaustion. Ye'll master every stroke and parry of the knife and dagger in order to defend yerself against our mortal enemy, the Amandán. And ye'll learn, ye will, the long history of our people."

They stared at each other, Finn conscious of his pulse pounding under Gideon's fingertips. After a moment, the Knight let go and sat back.

"And if ye manage to survive yer apprenticeship, then ye'll be a true warrior of the Tuatha De Danaan."

Finn blinked, not sure what to say. He jumped when Gideon abruptly rose.

"Now, to yer first task." Gideon led the way to the front door, pausing to snag the tin pail from the wooden crate. "Here. Ye'll need this."

"What's it for?"

"One of yer many chores will be to harvest the deadnettle leaves. They are more effective when fresh, especially if we are making a poultice or salve, or for a curative tea."

Finn took the pail and headed outside. As he started down the steps, Gideon grabbed his arm and jerked him backwards.

"Are ye daft? *Never* leave our house without taking a look about ye. Assume the Amandán are always hunting us. Remember, the slaughter of every living De Danaan drives them, day and night."

"But aren't crows supposed to warn us if any Amandán are nearby?"

"They are. But only short-lived warriors depend entirely on those trickster birds. So, be mindful of yer surroundings."

"Yes, sir."

They scanned the yard and the street beyond. Gideon kept one hand on the handle of the knife behind his back. After a minute, the Knight gave a nod. They walked down the steps and across the yard to the hedge.

"I wonder why we call it *dead*nettle when it helps us heal." Finn crouched down and eyed the sharp spines on the stalks.

Gideon took a knee next to him. "'Tis more commonly known as the *slainte* nettle."

"*Slawn-che?*" Finn said, mimicking the Knight's pronunciation.

"*Slainte* means 'health' in Gaelic. A fitting title for a plant that does so much for us De Danaan. From a tea to promote swift healing to a paste for wounds and even broken bones, the *slainte* nettle is as important to our people as our weapons. Now, watch." He reached over and gingerly took a leaf between finger and thumb and plucked it. "The trick to avoiding the spines on the stems, as well as the tiny pricklies along the edges, is to grasp the leaf in the dead center." He dropped the first one in the bucket sitting between them and stood up. "I want this pail overflowing before dinner."

"It's going to take a lot of leaves to fill it."

"Aye, that it will. Ye best get started." He rose to his feet and left.

An hour later, Finn straightened with a groan. He worked the kinks out of his back as he peered around the neighborhood. *I wonder if any mortals know about us.*

Picking up the full bucket, he started for the house. His fingers smarted from the nettles, and his face and arms were reddened from sunburn. As he reached the steps, he flinched, almost dropping the pickings when a voice spoke from the shadowy corner of the porch.

"All finished, then?"

"Yeah. I mean, yes, sir." Finn held out the pail as he joined his master. Gideon sat in a decrepit lawn chair, a knife across his knees. "Have you been there all this time?"

"Aye."

"Why?"

Gideon stood up. He peered into the pail as he took it and gave a nod of approval. "Why do ye think?" Without another word, he went inside.

Four

Pulling on a tee shirt over hair still damp from his morning shower, Gideon stepped out of his bedroom. Silent even in work boots, he crossed the hall to Finn's open door and leaned inside. Pre-dawn shadows filled the room. A faint whiffling sound came from the mound of covers on the narrow bed.

"Wake, Finnegan." He waited for any sign of life. There was a slight hitch in breathing from the mound, then nothing. "'Tis time to go."

Something stirred. Then a bare foot poked out from under the cover.

"Now, boyo."

The foot wiggled at him in annoyance.

Gideon cocked an eyebrow. Stepping closer, he grabbed Finn by the ankle; he hesitated for a moment. But only for a moment.

Then dragged him off the mattress.

Well-cushioned by the comforter wrapped around him, Finn hit the floor with a thump. Breathless from shock, he stared up open-mouthed, his face a pale oval in the dim light.

The Knight grinned back. "'Tis certain someone forgot lesson number one from yesterday. When I say move, I mean move."

Twenty minutes later, Finn sat in the truck's passenger seat, still munching on a slice of buttered toast. Pressing his cheek against the cold glass of the window, he swallowed the last bite and stared up at the towering sandstone cliffs flying past him on either side of the narrow road. Their reddish color was muted in the headlights of Gideon's pickup.

I can't believe it's finally happening, Finn thought. He jiggled a leg, heel tapping against the floorboard as he fought to calm the butterflies in his stomach. "What's this park called again?" he asked over the rumble of the engine.

"'Garden of the Gods,'" Gideon said. The truck bounced about as he pulled off the main road onto a graveled shoulder. The engine died with a shudder and a clunk. "'Tis a natural park and wilderness area owned by the city. It runs for miles and is quite popular with rock climbers and hikers." He smiled to himself. "And others."

"Is the spot far?" Finn asked as they clambered out, Gideon holding two knives. He glanced around. In the pale light, misshapen sandstone formations looked like frozen monsters, with scrub oaks and pine trees for arms.

Tucking one blade into the leather sheath behind him, the Knight stuck the other through the belt at his hip. With a grunt, he pushed the door shut with one shoulder, the hinges squealing. "No, not the site I've picked out. And 'tis secluded, so I doubt we'll have any unwanted spectators, especially at this early hour." He zipped up his canvas jacket. "Come along."

They left the road and followed a path winding westward through a maze of boulders and trees. After a few minutes of steady going, Gideon veered north and began climbing up a steep gully.

Finn labored to keep up, feet sinking into the gully's sandy bottom. *It's like hiking with a Marine.* He sighed in relief when they emerged on top of a stony ridge, crowned with a scattering of juniper trees. Their spicy scent filled the air.

"Just in time," Gideon said, looking across the city to the eastern plains beyond. He glanced over at Finn. Taking the boy's shoulders, he repositioned him, angling him due east. "Stand ready, now."

"Yes, sir." Finn pulled his father's stone out of the pocket of his hoodie and squeezed it tight in one fist, eyes locked on the horizon. When the first sliver of light appeared, he held the rock up to the rising sun and began chanting the ancient words of the Song.

"I am a wind on the sea,
I am a wave of the ocean,
I am the roar of the sea,
I am a bull of seven battles,
I am a hawk on the cliff,
I am a teardrop of sunlight,
I am a gentle herb,
I am a boar enraged,
I am a salmon in a pool,
I am a lake in a plain,
I am the vigor of man
I am the meaning of poetry,
I am a spear on the attack, pouring forth combat,
I am the god who fires your mind."

As Finn spoke the final words, the sun spilled over the rim of the earth. It threw blue shadows to the west; a warm breeze kissed his face. His arm vibrated with the thumping of his heart as he waited. A moment passed, then another.

Nothing happened.

Finn swallowed, his mouth suddenly dry. He peeked over at the Knight's face.

Gideon stood frowning, one eye on the mounting sun as he stared at Finn's upraised hand. "Hand me yer stone, lad."

Finn passed it over. "Maybe I said the words wrong?"

"No, ye recited them well enough." He closed a fist around the moonstone. Pale light oozed between his fingers. "'Tis odd—it's working now. Here, try it again." The stone's brilliance faded when he passed it back. They both held their breath as Finn lifted his arm once more, knuckles white.

Nothing happened.

Again.

Finn dropped his hand in defeat. A voice, sounding a great deal like his cousin, jeered in his head. *Hey, Halfer Boy! Why are you still carrying your da's stone around? Think maybe some of* our *mojo might rub off on it? Maybe even light it up for you when the time comes?* Cruel laughter followed.

He clenched his jaw. *I should've known it wouldn't work. I was stupid to think it would.* Afraid to look at the Knight, afraid of seeing disappointment (or worse, disgust), he stared at the horizon. *Why can't something turn out* right *for me? Just for once?*

Before he could stop it, the frustration and self-pity turned to anger. It spilled from his gut and spread throughout his body. Sweat broke out on his face and back. *Oh, crap, not this, not now.* He fought for control as Gideon spoke.

"Well, now, that's something I've not seen before."

"Is it because I'm half mortal?" Finn said between gritted teeth. He dug his nails into his palms, trying to halt the storm building up inside.

"Possibly. But that doesn't mean—"

"How am I supposed to fight them if I can't recognize them?" he asked, his voice breaking. "How am I supposed to see the Amandáns' true forms if my moonstone doesn't work?"

"There are many ways to battle those beasties. And shortly, I'll teach ye how to—"

"How to what?" Finn cut him off again. "*Smell* for them? Like a dog?"

"Finnegan, the moonstone is only one of our weapons." Gideon tried again, his own face darkening. "And if ye'll stop bleedin' interrupting me, I'll explain—"

Finn ignored him. He stalked over to the edge of the cliff, legs both stiff and shaky at the same time, and looked down at the tip of a lone pine. A violent fury deafened him to Gideon's voice. The fury that spun him out of control every time.

And into a red place that frightened him.

Dumbass rock! I should have thrown it away a long time ago. The anger flared. A black rage so thick he could almost spit it out onto the ground. His mouth twisting into an ugly mask, he cocked his arm back.

A hand caught his wrist. "Oh, no, ye don't. None of that, now." Before Finn could stop him, Gideon pried his fist open and dug out the stone, still keeping a grip with his other hand.

"Let go of me!" Finn flung himself back, eyes wild and his feet scrambling in the gravely dirt for purchase. He clawed at Gideon's fingers, trying to pry them off, his own chewed nails leaving shallow gouges along the Knight's knuckles. Dark red spots flickered at the edge of his vision.

His feet left the ground momentarily when Gideon yanked him closer, until they stood nose to nose. Shocked by the bruising grip around his wrist, he blinked, the red haze lessening.

"We Celts," Gideon growled softly, his Irish brogue deepening. "Be we De Danaan or mortal, are famous for our tempers. And some, like meself, are gifted with more than our fair share. So, I suggest ye rein yers in, boyo, before *I* get angry." He waited for a long minute. "Let it go, lad. Let the rage go or 'twill be a black hobgoblin riding yer back all yer long life. I would know. And we've enough monsters to battle as it is."

After a few moments, Finn sucked in a shaky breath, his body strung tighter than a new wire fence. He swallowed, and swallowed again, then nodded at Gideon. As the Knight released him, he stepped back, rubbing his wrist, his chest heaving. Tremors shook him as the last of the rage faded. Taking another breath, he leaned over and rested his hands on his knees.

"T'was a fine display of the warp spasm."

Finn straightened up and blew his sweaty hair off his forehead. "The...the what?"

"The warp spasm. 'Tis the battle rage that sweeps through all Celts, De Danaan and mortals, in times of stress or strong emotion. Ye've experienced it before, I take it?"

"Yeah, but I thought it was just...you know, being really pissed off."

"Aye, that's one way to describe it. And although it can be difficult to control, it's bleedin' useful in a fight."

It's bleedin' freaky is what it is, Finn thought. He looked up in surprise when Gideon held out an open hand, the stone resting on his palm.

"Now, shall I keep this for ye? Or would ye care to have it back?"

Finn hesitated, then reached over. "I'll keep it." He tucked it back into his pocket, then slumped on a nearby boulder and rested his elbows on his knees. "So, what happens now?" *He's going to send me back, I just know it. Well, I don't blame him—what Knight would want a halfer apprentice anyway?*

Gideon pulled out both knives. He wagged one of them at Finn. "Why, we complete the ceremony, of course."

Finn's head whipped up. His mouth sagged opened as he watched his master turn and stride along the crest of the ridge. The Knight halted, after several yards, in front of a dead pine tree, its trunk blackened from a long-ago lightning storm. He glanced over his shoulder with a frown.

"Finnegan," he barked. "Move yer arse." As Finn joined him, he cuffed him lightly on the side of the head. "Do not make me repeat an order."

"Yes, sir."

"Take this." He held out one of the knives to Finn, handle first.

Finn grasped it. He hefted it a few times, surprised at the weight of such a graceful form. The well-oiled metal gleamed like a bronze flame; its color was an identical match to his hair. "What do I do with this?"

Gideon pointed at a jagged limb poking out from the side of the pine. "Throw yer blade at the junction between the branch and trunk."

"I'm not very good at this."

"Do yer best."

"Okay," Finn said doubtfully. He pulled back an arm. Squinting at the branch, he aimed and threw. The knife wobbled through the air. It smacked sideways against the tree and dropped to the ground. He sighed. "And my day just gets better and better."

Gideon ignored the comment. "Now, once more." He handed Finn the second blade. "This time, choose a line from the Song that reflects what ye need to be."

"What I need to be?"

"Aye. Repeat the line over and over. Aloud."

"Why?"

"Ye will see."

This is so lame, Finn thought. He ran through the Song in his mind. "'I am a spear on the attack, pouring forth combat,'" he muttered self-consciously.

As his fingers closed around the knife's grip, the worn leather silky against his palm, Finn felt a pull like a river's current run from his chest and down his arm to his hand. The hairs on the back of his neck stiffened. Taking a deep breath, he cocked his arm again. "'I am a spear on the attack, pouring forth combat,'" he repeated. With a flick of elbow and wrist, he hurled the second blade toward the target.

Thunk! Dried pine needles showered down when the blade buried itself in the tree. It stuck there, quivering, sunlight dancing along the bronze.

Finn whirled around and stared wide-eyed at his master. "H-how did I...?"

"The words of our Song are powerful magic, boyo. They strengthen and enhance our abilities, especially in battle. That's why the ancient peoples, both human and De Danaan, honored bards so highly. The druids of words." Gideon gestured toward the tree. "Fetch yer weapons."

Finn jogged over and retrieved the blades. "Can I try that again?" he asked as he rejoined his master.

Gideon shook his head. He took the knives and slid them back into his belt. "No, now we must face a repulsive task. One I've been dreading since yesterday." He laid a hand on Finn's shoulder. "Brace yerself, lad."

 Five

"C'mon! Do I have to?" Finn grimaced when Gideon handed him several pairs of folded jeans of various sizes.

"Aye, ye do." Gideon pointed to a nearby dressing room. "Spending an afternoon at Wal-Mart is not the way I planned to celebrate both the ceremony and yer birthday, but ye're woefully lacking." He checked the price tag on one of the jeans, then pulled out his wallet and thumbed through the bills. "We can afford two, plus a few shirts." *And another pair of shoes,* he thought, glancing down at the boy's feet. *Although he'll most likely out*grow *them before he out*wears *them.* "And what about…?" Gideon's voice trailed off as he gestured vaguely toward Finn's middle region.

Finn glanced down in confusion. "What about…*what?*"

"Underwear."

"You mean, like…like…am I wearing *any?*" Finn's voice cracked with thirteen year old boy indignation.

Gideon fought a smile. And lost. "No, ye dolt. Do ye need more?"

"I guess," Finn mumbled, blushing as red as his hair. He ducked inside the dressing room. With one last glare, he pulled the door closed with a snick.

Laughing softly under his breath, the Knight pressed against a rack of shirts as he attempted to stay out of the way of the other shoppers packing the aisles. He watched as Finn emerged a few minutes later and stood in front of the full-length mirror, tugging at the waistband of the jeans.

"And just what are ye doing?"

"Getting them right. They don't sag enough." Finn pulled up his tee shirt to check the fit.

"I can see the top of yer boxers." Gideon stepped closer to shield Finn as two teenage girls walked past. "As can everyone else."

"Yeah, that's the point." Finn examined himself in the mirror, then looked up. "What?"

"No."

"No? Why? Gideon, this is how *everyone* dresses. We're supposed to fit in with human society, right?"

"Mine are not on display, and I've manage to blend in," Gideon declared. "For quite some time now."

"That's because you're an adult."

"And thus lack any sense of fashion?"

"Well, yeah. I mean, yes, sir." Finn headed back to the dressing room, then paused. "Have you ever had an apprentice before?"

Grief poked a claw into Gideon's heart. "Aye. 'Twas long ago."

"Well, teenagers dress a lot different these days. In fact, teenagers *act* a lot different these days, too." Turning around, Finn stumbled on the hem of the too-long pant legs. He lurched into a clothes rack and knocked it over with a crash. Hangers skittered across the tile floor.

The corner of the Knight's mouth twitched. "Why, of course, they do."

"Here, take these." Gideon handed the plastic bags of clothes to Finn as they left the store. "I'll get the food." They made their way through the overflowing parking lot. Their truck was squeezed into the furthest corner, behind several behemoth campers. Thunder rumbled overhead as a spring storm darkened the sky. Rain clouds bunched up and spilled over the mountain range west of the city, turning the day gloomy. A car rolling past, searching for an empty spot, flipped on its headlights.

"Our afternoon deluge is a wee earlier," Gideon said as they approached their vehicle. He tossed the keys over to Finn. "We best put everything inside the cab." He shook his head when the keys sailed past the boy's outstretched hand and skittered under one of the recreational vehicles.

"Nice throw," Finn muttered. He dropped his bags by the passenger door and jogged over to the RV.

Crouching down by its folding steps, he stretched out an arm. The reek of a septic system in desperate need of emptying assaulted his nose. His fingers scrabbled across the asphalt as he tried to fish the keys closer. A fat drop of rain splashed the back of his neck.

At that moment, a hoarse caw split the air. Finn twisted his head around. A crow stood on the top step, its claws scraping against the aluminum tread. Boy and bird eyed each other. Before Finn could move, the crow shook out its damp feathers and flapped away.

"Um ... excuse me? Could you help me?" asked a soft voice behind him.

Finn jumped, banging an elbow on the undercarriage. Cursing under his breath, he scooted out from under the RV and stood up. A teenage girl stood nearby, the increasing drizzle softening the curls in her brown hair.

"Oh, I'm sorry," she said. "I didn't mean to scare you, but could you tell me if there's a bus stop nearby?" She edged closer, a gentle smile curving her lips. Droplets glittered on the tips of her sweeping eyelashes, framing hazel eyes. Thunder boomed again as the rain began falling harder.

Finn found himself smiling back with a loopy grin. Keys forgotten, he wiped his hands on his jeans. "I don't know, but I can ask my—"

A pale beam shot over his shoulder and spotlighted the girl's face. With a snarl, she flung up an arm. Her features began twisting and shifting with a moist popping sound. Her head jerked back and forth. Finn gasped, unable to move.

Stabbed by the light from Gideon's moonstone, the Amandán groaned. Its pelt rippled as it transformed into a distorted half-ape, half-human shape. Snapping its jaw, it shook itself like a dog, water spraying from mossy green fur.

"Ah, fresh meat," the creature grunted, curling its lips back in a yellow-toothed grin. As Finn stood frozen with shock, it stretched black-tipped fingers toward his face.

Something grabbed the collar of his shirt and yanked him backwards.

"Are ye trying to hold hands with the bleedin' thing?" Gideon thrust him to one side. "Now, watch and learn, boyo." The light faded when the Knight shoved the stone in his pocket. His bronze blade was a blur in the rain as he slashed and stabbed at the goblin. He drove it back, trapping it against the side of the camper. "Fetch the other weapon whilst I keep it occupied," he called over the roar of the downpour. "Hurry!"

Finn dove under the RV and lunged for the keys. Scrambling to his feet, he rushed to their truck. His hands shook as he fumbled to unlock the door. Jerking it open, he scrabbled under the seat, grabbed the weapon, and raced back. He shook wet hair out of his eyes and took a stance beside his master, worry worms squirming in his gut. The knife felt heavy and awkward in his hand. As he watched, the creature swayed back and forth, flinching away from the burning touch of the Knight's blade.

"So, ye've come to pick a fight, have ye?" Gideon said. "And just when will ye manky beasts realize Eire is lost to ye forever? And that ye will never win this war?"

"'Twill be ours again," the Amandán snarled back. "Right after we spit out the bones of all De Danaan and their mortal allies." It made a rude gesture. "Invaders. Thieves of our earth."

"Ye should have fought harder, then, to hold the green land."

With its mouth stretched in rage, the Amandán lunged at the Knight, hissing, "*Poc sídhe.*" Its fingertips whispered past the Knight's face.

Gideon jerked his head back just in time. Feinting to one side, he dodged under the goblin's reach. "'I am a boar enraged,'" he shouted as he came in low and buried his blade in the Amandán's chest. Lightning cracked overhead and drowned out the creature's shriek. Gideon leaped back. He grabbed Finn and whirled around, shielding the boy with his body.

The Amandán exploded. It sprayed the back of Gideon's work shirt with gray-green ash and vanished. The knife clattered to the ground.

Finn sucked in a shaky breath as Gideon released him. He turned around and stared at the mound of powder a few feet away, his heart hammering against his ribs. "Is-is it dead?" He hoped his master didn't notice his voice cracking.

"Oh, 'tis not dead." Gideon bent over and picked up the weapon. He held it between thumb and finger to rinse it off in the diminishing rainfall, the cloudburst as quick to leave as to arrive. "Amandán are almost impossible to kill. All I've done is weakened it. 'Twill take some time for that one to gain enough strength to reform and attack again."

Finn stepped closer and poked at the sodden mess with his toe. The rain was already washing away the traces of left-over goblin. He grimaced. "*Bleh*, that stuff stinks!" He waved a hand in front of his nose. "Smells like burnt rubber."

"Aye, it does. Which is why an apprentice with even a modicum of intelligence would not stick his bleedin' shoe in it."

While Finn scratched his head, trying to determine if he had been insulted, Gideon walked over to the truck and rummaged through the storage bin in the back, finally locating a rag. With a few swipes, he dried the blade and slid it back into its sheath, under the tail of his shirt.

"Quite a beginning to yer apprenticeship, eh?" He propped an elbow on the side of the truck bed. His blue eyes twinkled as he wiped wet ash from his cheek. It left a smear across his lean face.

Finn grinned back weakly and nodded, his pulse slowing. He gathered the plastic bags still sitting by the passenger side and tossed them into the cab, then joined the Knight.

For a few minutes, they stood side by side, watching the storm clouds race eastward. Around them, shoppers emerged from their cars, having waited out the storm before heading to the store.

After a moment, Finn wrinkled his nose and sniffed. Trying to act nonchalant, he eased away from the goblin puddle.

Gideon slipped off his shirt. "Best get used to the stench, boyo." Holding it out, he examined the stained material. "A good scrubbing and 'twill be respectable again."

Finn nodded. His eyes widened when he noticed a Celtic knot tattooed on the swell of muscle of the Knight's right arm, just below the sleeve of his master's tee. The green lines of the sigil wove in and out, around and back, in a pattern with no beginning or ending. A wisp of a memory washed over him. A memory of a similar tattoo on his father's arm. "My da had one," he said, almost to himself.

"Did he? The mark of Knighthood?"

"Yeah." Finn frowned. "My uncle's a Knight, too, but he doesn't have one."

"Yer da and Uncle Owen are of a younger generation of Tuatha De Danaan. Fergus was a rare one to have followed the old custom."

"Oh." Finn hesitated for a moment, then looked up at his master. "Just how old *are* you?"

"Thirty-seven," he said offhandedly. He tossed the shirt into the bed before heading for the cab. Finn trotted around to the other side and climbed in.

As the truck coughed to life, Gideon glanced over. "I best teach ye how to remove goblin remains from yer clothing. We'll begin with me shirt."

"Me? Why do I have to do it? It's not mine."

"I dinna write the rules. It clearly states in the 'How to Train Yer Apprentice' manual that the apprentice does the laundry."

"Can I see this manual? When we get back?"

"I seem to recall that I've misplaced me copy."

"So, how do I know you're not just making all this sh—crap up?"

"Because I am Gideon Lir, Knight of the Tuatha De Danaan," he proclaimed in a solemn voice. "And our word and our honor are the one and the same."

Finn muttered something under his breath that rhymed with "*ghoul skit*" as they rolled out the parking lot and headed for home.

The Journal of Finnegan MacCullen: May 22

This is so lame!!! And I hope Gideon reads this so he knows I think this is totally unfair and stupid!! And lame!!!

Guys don't do journals. It's so...so girly! What does a warrior need a journal for, anyway?

Gideon told me...no, wait...*ordered* me to write down what I learn each day. He said starting it on my thirteenth birthday would mean a lot to me when I got older. And then he told me that he still keeps one.

Wow, like *that's* something to brag about?

<u>What I Learned Today:</u>

Amandán means *Fool* in old Gaelic (the language of the Celts).

They sometimes trick (or fool) us and also mortals by taking on the appearance of a person or some other object. That's so they can get closer and kill us. They can't hold the shape very long, which is good, because then we'd be *really* screwed when it came to hunting them.

They believe in this ancient legend that, if they kill every single De Danaan in the world, then they can return home to Ireland and reclaim it. Which doesn't makes sense to me. I mean, don't they know there's like six million humans living in Ireland??? I don't think *they're* going to be too happy sharing the island with stinky green goblins with bad breath.

Amandán kill with the *poc sidhe*. If they touch your face or head with their fingers, it gives you a cerebral hemorrhage. What humans call a stroke. That's what *poc sidhe* means: fey stroke. Gideon pronounces it *poke she*.

We got an Amandán today. Well, Gideon got it. I just watched. It was a lot bigger and faster than I had imagined. A lot smellier, too.

A lot scarier, too.

The ceremony totally sucked. My stone wouldn't work. But I did okay with the knife. He told me De Danaan used to use swords and spears more, in the old days, but it got too hard to hide them under our clothes around humans. Now, we just use knives and daggers. Makes sense.

Gideon just came by and told me I can sleep in tomorrow morning because we're going to be up late doing some training tomorrow night. That's good, because I'm fried already!

And it's only my first day.

This is going to be a lot harder than I'd thought.

The Journal of Gideon Lir: May 22

Ye gods.

Never in all these centuries of battling the beasties have I witnessed such a bold attack by an Amandán. My instincts tell me that something is amiss. What it is, I do not know, but I've not lived all these years (thirty-seven decades, to be exact—I did not lie to the boy) without listening to my instincts.

And it seems Finnegan has been granted a generous share of the Celtic temper—something we have in common, to be sure. His warp spasm caught us both by surprise. It was all I could do to keep *mine* under control.

But the lad did well with the Song—and he has a fine, tenor voice. The words sang through him like a true Tuatha De Danaan when he used his weapon. Regretfully, his mortal blood prevents him from using the moonstone's magic.

And not just any moonstone, but his da's. It is a sorrow for him, although he tries to hide it.

Six

"Unbelievable." Gideon shook his head as he stared across the kitchen table.

"What is?" Finn asked, cheeks bulging with shepherd's pie as he sat hunched over his meal.

"Yer manners. Or lack of." Gideon reached across and pushed Finn's elbows off the table. As the boy straightened, he added, "And ease up. Ye needn't wolf yer food like that. I'm not going to thieve yer dinner."

"Sorry. Bad habit." Finn scraped the bowl and licked his spoon clean. He looked over at the stove. "Can I have some more?"

"*May* I have some more." Gideon corrected him. "And yes, of course. As I've said before, this is yer home now." He waved a hand around the room. The last rays of the late-afternoon sun warmed the kitchen while a green-scented breeze wafted through the open window over the sink.

"Thanks!" Finn hopped up and headed over to the stove. He filled his bowl to the rim with chunks of beef and vegetables, and then topped it off with a generous dollop of mashed potatoes. He hesitated, then added a second spoonful. "I like this," he said over his shoulder.

"Shepherd's pie?"

"No. Well, yeah, the pie's good." He sat back down. "I mean, having extra."

"Extra?"

"You know. Extra food. Extra room."

"Things were a bit tight, eh? At yer aunt and uncle's?"

Finn nodded as he dug in. "We always had enough. But never *more*. Sometimes, they kind of forgot...me."

For a brief moment, Gideon saw the hurt dart across Finn's face, the faint scattering of freckles across his nose standing out against his pale skin. The hurt of being the unwanted one, the mixed breed in a family of pure bloods. The additional burden on an already overburdened family.

If I offer any comfort or sympathy, he'll take it all wrong, Gideon thought. "Well, I'd eat hearty, if I were ye. We'll begin training right after supper. As soon as ye're finished washing the dishes." He rose and carried his own bowl over to the sink. "And no bemoaning yer fate as an overworked apprentice."

Finn grinned and thumped his chest. "Bring it!"

Oh, gods, I'm dying, Finn thought, leg muscles burning from fatigue. His knees folded beneath him, and he slumped to the ground. Sweat stung his eyes. *I can't do any more of those leaps.* He swallowed back bile when the shepherd's pie tried to make an encore. *Bleh! Why did I eat so much at dinner?* He groaned when a hand grabbed him under the arm and hauled him upright.

"On yer feet, boyo."

"Oh, come on, Gideon." Finn blew out a breath in exasperation, then pulled up his shirt and wiped his face. "I'm never going to be able to make it." Looking around their backyard, he flung his arms apart. "And it's getting dark out here. Can't I just try it again tomorrow?"

Gideon gazed up at the spring evening, delighting in the stars. "Tis a soft evening for late May, to be sure. And we'll be out here enjoying it all night until ye make one successful jump. Just one. Then we can both retire." He pointed to the far end of the yard. "'Once more unto the breach,'" he quoted, then added, "Now, that would be a line from Shakespeare."

"But I thought you hated the English," Finn said as they walked over to the stone wall. "Being Irish and all."

"I do. But the Bard is another thing altogether." He amended after a moment, "Except for *A Midsummer Night's Dream.*"

"Why's that?"

"His interpretation of the Fey."

"Pretty bad?"

"Aye. Ye should read it, just to understand how mortals view us."

Finn nodded politely. *Read Shakespeare—yeah, like that's ever going to happen.*

Standing with his back to the wall, Gideon gestured toward the house. "Aim for the space on the roof between the two dormers. What words are ye chanting?"

"'I am a wind on the sea.' But I don't think it's working for me." Finn frowned. "Maybe I should try another line from the Song?"

"I would."

Finn chewed on his lip as he pondered. The night breeze brushed past his cheek, bringing the scent of wood smoke from a neighbor's chimney. He stared up at the roof. "'I am a hawk on the cliff.'"

A jolt of *something* zinged through the soles of his feet and moved up his legs. Taking a deep breath, he straightened, eyes fixed on the shingles. "'I am a hawk on the cliff,'" he repeated. The feeling intensified, growing like a storm racing down the mountainside before attacking the plains east of the city.

He crouched low, still chanting, then shot forward. Arms and legs pumping, he picked up speed. Halfway across the yard, he gave a cry and flung himself into the air. Instead of falling back to earth, he rose higher and higher, his mouth stretched wide in wonder.

With a thump, he landed on the roof.

Clutching the edge of the dormer, he wobbled a moment before catching his balance. "Ye gods!" he gasped in an unconscious imitation of his master. He spun around and beamed down at Gideon. "Did you see that?" he shouted. "Did you see what I did? That was so freaking awesome!" He punched a fist into the air, almost losing his footing. "Oops."

"*Gle mhaith.*" Gideon strolled across the yard, hands stuffed into his jeans pockets and a look of relief on his face. "But lower yer voice, boyo. Even through we're secluded back here, the neighbors might become alarmed."

Finn nodded and squatted down on his heels, still grinning ear to ear. "What does *glay moth* mean?"

"It means 'very good' or 'well done' in Gaelic."

"*Gle mhaith,*" he repeated, practicing it a few times. After a few minutes, he scratched his head as he glanced around. "Um...Gideon?"

"Yes?"

"So, how do I get down?"

"Now, why would ye want to do a thing like that? Ye've only just got up there. After dozens of attempts." Gideon waved a hand. "Revel in yer success." He continued toward the house. "Well, I'm off to bed."

As Finn listened in disbelief, the back door closed with a snick. For a long minute, the sound of crickets serenaded the evening.

"Gideon?"

The crickets chirped louder.

Uh-uh—no way. He's not going to leave me stuck up here all night, Finn thought. *Or is he?* He dropped to his bottom and stretched his legs out. *Maybe this is a test, too, and I'm supposed to figure out what to do next.*

Leaning forward, he peered at the ground. *Maybe I could hang from the gutter and drop down.* He inched forward, trying to work up the nerve. *Man, that's a long ways down there.*

He jumped when the window next to him flew open with a bang.

Gideon stuck his head out. "We'll tackle landing in the morning." He waved Finn in, moving to one side as the boy clambered past. "Shower, and then to bed."

Fifteen minutes later, Finn crawled under his covers. He yawned as he stretched his back and legs. The bedside lamp cast a warm glow around the room. Even after only a few days, it felt like home in a way his aunt and uncle's house never quite had. Maybe because he had always had to share a room and wear hand-me-down clothes. And struggle for hand-me-down attention.

Clasping his hands behind damp hair, he gazed at the ceiling, reliving the feeling of the Song thrumming through him. *Gideon was right—words* are *powerful magic.*

The sound of humming drifted through his half-opened door. Lifting his head off the pillow, Finn listened to Gideon moving about his own room across the hall. After a few moments, the Knight broke into song.

"*The minstrel boy to the war has gone,*" sang Gideon softly in a fine, rich voice. "*In the ranks of death, ye shall find him; His father's sword he has girded on, and his wild harp slung behind him.*" The voice faded to humming, then stopped.

There was a footstep, then a soft tap on his door. Finn grinned, secretly pleased his master always wished him good night. *Mom and Da used to do that,* he thought.

Gideon stuck his head in. "*Codladh sumh,* Finn." He started to close the door, then paused. "And excellent job, boyo, writing in yer journal each day. I thank ye for keeping yer word." With a smile, he left, shutting the door behind him.

Finn groaned to himself. *I forgot to do my journal! My stupid, dumb butt, what-a-total-waste-of-time journal.* He sighed. *I'm too tired. I'll just do it in the morning.* He rolled over, turned off the bedside lamp, and burrowed deeper under the comforter.

For a few moments, he lay gazing into the darkness, curling and uncurling his toes. Guilt tapped on his shoulder. *I know, I know. I promised him that I'd do it every day.* He turned the lamp back on and stared across the room at the new ledger on the desk, its brown cover almost invisible in the dim light. It's a long ways over there. *I know—I'll do* two *entries tomorrow to make up for it.* With a nod, he turned off the lamp.

The lamp turned on.

And off.

And on.

Muttering cuss words that would have gotten him a ringing clout on the head, as well as extra chores for a week, Finn flung aside the covers. Padding on bare feet to the desk, he grabbed the journal and stomped back to the bed. He tucked his legs under the still-warm comforter and opened the book to the next blank page. As he wrote, his lips moved silently, practicing the Gaelic phrase he had learned. The scratching of the pen filled the room.

Outside the door, Gideon stood in the hallway, his head cocked as he listened. "*Gle mhaith*," he murmured, then headed downstairs.

even

Finn peered in the bathroom mirror at his tousled mess of red hair. He wet his fingers and tried to plaster a lock over his widow's peak. No such luck.

Giving up, he headed out of the bathroom, picked up a tee shirt off the bedroom floor, and gave it a sniff. *Not too bad*, he thought, and tugged it on over his head. He started to leave, then paused to grab his stone off the nightstand. "Don't know why I still carry this thing around," he muttered, tucking it in his pocket. *Because it was Da's.* Ignoring the voice in his head, he left and headed downstairs to the kitchen.

"I was about to serve ye breakfast in bed," Gideon said, stirring a pot of oatmeal at the stove. Bacon sizzled and sputtered in a nearby frying pan.

"R-really?"

"What do ye think?"

"Uh—no." Finn scrunched up his face as he studied his master. "You're being sarcastic, aren't you, sir?"

"Why, no, not at all," said Gideon. Sarcastically. He glanced over his shoulder. "Say, dinna ye wear that shirt yesterday?" His eyes traveled up to the boy's head. "And ye are in desperate need of a hair cut."

"I like my hair like this. It hides my thing."

"Yer *thing?*"

"You know." Finn walked over to the Knight and pushed his hair off his forehead. "See? It looks like I got a tiny horn growing out of the center of my head."

Gideon chuckled. "Well, I never thought about it that way. I suppose ye'll just have to stay shaggy." He gave the pot another stir and flipped off the burner. "Set the table."

Finn bustled about, locating the mismatched dishes. He took the platter of bacon from Gideon and placed it on the table. Breaking off a piece, he popped it into his mouth with a porky crunch. "What are we doing today?"

"What we've been doing all week. And what we'll do most every day of yer apprenticeship." Gideon ladled steaming cereal into both bowls with a *plop*, then joined him at the table. "Fitness training, at least one history lesson, and chores. And we'll begin weapon training today. Ye learned the fundamentals alongside yer cousins, I assume?"

"Well...kind of. So, when do we hunt Amandán?" Finn poured milk over the oatmeal and dug in. After a bite, he added a generous spoonful of brown sugar from the small crock on the table.

Gideon picked up his mug of tea. Taking a sip, he peered over the rim at Finn. "Not until ye've mastered the basic skills to me satisfaction. Hunting should never be taken lightly. Even experienced De Danaan have lost their lives fighting the beasties."

Finn nodded. *Like my parents*, he thought. Memories of the last time he'd ever seen them flooded his mind, memories of a red-headed man swinging him high in the air, his eyes more blue than the sky. A voice filled with laughter. A fall of soft brown hair appearing next to them, stirred by a breeze. A woman's delicate voice and the scent of lemon soap as she kissed him goodbye.

With an effort, Finn slammed his inner eye closed, shattering the vision. He forced himself to take a few more bites before giving up and pushing the bowl away, his appetite gone. "So, how come we don't just have one big battle? Us versus them. Winner takes all."

"Why, for one thing, they outnumber us by a hundredfold." Gideon said, plowing through his own cereal. "And, there's more to our long war with the Amandán than ye know. 'Tis not just *us versus them*. Mortals play a role, to some degree." He pointed a spoon at Finn's bowl. "Eat."

"I'm not hungry."

"Then ye'll be enjoying cold oatmeal for lunch. We cannot afford to waste food."

With a scowl, Finn pulled his bowl back and began picking at his breakfast. "What did you mean by "mortals play a role"?"

Gideon drained the last of the tea, then rose and carried his dishes to the sink. He began rummaging through a drawer. "Best leave the history lesson for this afternoon. Now, hand me yer belt."

Finn's stomach lurched. "Why? I'm eating as fast as..." His voice trailed off when the Knight turned around, a leather knife sheath in one hand. "Oh." With a silent sigh of relief, he stood up, unfastened his belt, and handed it over.

"Yer to be armed at all times," Gideon said as he slid the sheath onto Finn's belt. "Never leave this house without a weapon."

"Yes, sir." He took his belt back. As he refastened it, the Knight stepped into the living room. He returned a moment later with one of the smaller hunting knives. "Here. Finish yer breakfast, *all of it*, clean the kitchen, and then meet me out back."

Standing in the middle of the yard twenty minutes later, Finn watched as Gideon jammed the end of a thick plank as tall as himself into the ground and leaned it against the back wall. A crude outline of a goblin was drawn on it, the wood pitted and splintered, especially in the chest region.

Gideon backed up a few feet. Sliding a knife out of his belt, he motioned for Finn to join him. "Now, the most important thing to remember when battling an Amandán with a blade is to..." He paused, eyebrows raised as he waited for Finn to answer.

"Stick it with the sharp end?"

The Knight blinked. He scratched the back of his neck with the tip of the weapon and tried again. "The *second* most important thing to remember when battling an Amandán with a blade is to..."

"...never let go."

"Aye, never let go. And one way to practice that is to attack this board over and over, thrusting yer weapon as deep as ye can, then ripping it free as quick as ye can. Since this plank is tougher than the hide of an Amandán, ye'll develop not only speed, but muscle, too. Remember, whilst contact with bronze burns them, 'tis the stab of a bronze blade that destroys them. Or, at least, disintegrates them." He shifted his feet and faced the target, the blade held at waist height. "Now watch."

Balancing on the balls of his feet, Gideon began chanting in a low voice. Without warning, he lunged forward in a blur of motion. The blade flashed in the morning light as he plunged it into the left eye of the mock goblin. A splinter of wood flew upward as he yanked it out. A second lunge and thrust planted the knife less than an inch from the same spot. Still chanting, Gideon pulled it free. With a flick of his wrist, he flipped the blade over and caught it, hilt forward and blade back. He spun on his toes and drove his weapon blindly into the target now behind him, releasing the handle as he completed his rotation. He left it sticking out of the beast's eye.

"Whoa," breathed Finn. He stared at the knife buried halfway to the hilt in the plank.

"Fetch the weapon," Gideon said, breathing easily.

Finn walked over, grasped the handle, and pulled. Nothing happened. Bracing his other hand and a foot on the board, he tried again. This time, he managed to yank it loose. He studied the target. "I think I can do that."

"'Tis more difficult than it appears. Ye might not be successful yer first time."

"Can I at least try?"

"Stab away, then."

Holding the knife the way his master had, Finn squared his shoulders and began chanting. "'I am a spear on the attack.'" Crouching down slightly, he tightened his grip until his knuckles whitened. Then, with a grunt, he attacked.

Pain zinged up his arm from the impact. "Son of a goat," he cursed and let go of the handle. The knife wobbled in place for a moment, then fell to the ground. Shaking his throbbing wrist, he glared up at the Knight.

Gideon stepped closer and plucked the blade from the tall grasses fringing the wall. "Milk before meat."

"What's that mean?"

"It means we best begin with something a bit easier." Tucking the weapon away, he led the way over to the middle of the yard. They stopped in front of the burlap bag Finn had seen his first day here. "Arm yerself."

Finn reached behind and slid his knife free. "Now, what?"

"Lock yer hand tightly against the tang." Gideon re-positioned Finn's grip closer to the crosspiece separating the blade from the handle. "That way ye won't break a thumb if the beastie jerks suddenly. That being the beastie." He pointed to the bag cram-packed with balls of newspaper. Bare dirt surrounded the dummy in a wide circle. "When ye thrust, extend yer arm fully. *Bury* yer blade, but remember to hold tight." He took hold of a long rope attached to the overhead cable and stepped to one side.

Finn nodded. Taking a stance in front of the bag, he licked his lips. *Here goes nothing.* "'I am the roar of the sea,'" he whispered.

At first, nothing. Then pressure, like a mounting wave, surged through his back and shoulders. He bounced on his toes a few times; darting forward, he stabbed at the bag. The target twirled about, dodging his attack. It swung up in a looping arch when Gideon yanked on the guy rope.

Still chanting, he slashed again. The tip of his knife sliced a few strands before the bag spun out of range. Gritting his teeth, he lunged over and over, chasing it in a circle as it danced about. Dust puffed up around his ankles. For ten minutes, he stabbed and lunged and missed. Sweat began to trickle down his face, stinging his eyes.

"Are ye planning on waltzing with the Amandán?" Gideon teased.

"Stop moving it," he rasped, stumbling to a halt, his chest heaving. He forced frustration down a dry throat.

"Then quit mucking about and stick the bleedin' thing."

Maybe I'll just stick you instead, he thought, blood humming in his ears. He blew his hair out of his eyes as he stalked the target. The Knight jiggled the bag enticingly. With a sudden charge, he plunged the weapon into the sack. "Gotcha," he gasped, still holding the knife.

With a powerful tug, Gideon sent the bag flying; the movement ripped the blade out of the boy's hand. The knife flashed in the sunlight as it spun end over end across the yard and sailed over the stone wall. It vanished into a stand of scrub oak on the other side.

Finn whirled around. "You did that on purpose!"

"Why, 'tis certain. Do ye think an Amandán is going to meekly stand there, eager to take a blade in the chest?" Gideon let go of the rope and flexed his hands. "Go fetch yer weapon."

"Screw this crap," Finn muttered under his breath. He stomped over to the picnic table near the back door and sank down on the bench. Bending forward, he stretched out his shirt and wiped his sweaty face. He jumped when a shadow fell across him. Without warning, a hand grabbed his arm and yanked him back on his feet.

Dragging Finn by the back of his tee shirt, Gideon stalked across the yard to the fence, the boy's feet scarcely touching the ground. "Ye've a choice, Finnegan MacCullen. Climb over that wall and retrieve yer weapon. Or else."

"Or else what?" Finn struggled to free himself from Gideon's iron grip.

"Or else I pitch ye over. Head over arse."

Finn froze and stared up at his master's face.

Gideon narrowed his eyes.

"I-I think I'll go get that knife now."

"Ye've a strong sense of self-preservation." Gideon let go and nodded toward the wall.

Finn turned and jogged away, bypassing the wooden gate off to one side. He hoisted himself up, swung his legs over, and hopped down. Beyond the wall, the ground sloped away. It dropped into a wide ravine filled with thick underbrush and the occasional pine. He half-walked, half-slid down to the bottom.

Working his way through thick patches of scrub oak, he searched back and forth across the ravine. *Where's the stupid knife?* he thought as he pawed through last year's leaves, wondering if Gideon really would have thrown him over the wall. *Yup, he would have*, he finally decided. Crunching his way toward the other side of the gully, he began climbing the far side. He passed a lichen-covered boulder halfway up the slope.

The boulder twitched.

Lifting its head and unfolding from a crouch, the Amandán grinned. "*Poc sídhe*" it hissed, lunging at Finn, black-tipped fingers scrabbling for his face.

Gideon frowned as he watched Finn disappear over the wall. *Ye gods*, he thought, *I hope we don't butt heads his* entire *apprenticeship. The boy certainly has a short fuse.* He listened to the sounds of Finn searching for the knife. *Just like another fiery apprentice I could name*—Gideon chose to ignore the voice of his old master.

I must find a way to help Finnegan deal with that temper of his. Help him channel that energy into something more—

He stiffened at the sudden harsh caw and looked up.

The crow blasted past the Knight's head. Its yellow claws skimmed the wall before it dipped out of sight into the trees beyond.

"Finnegan!" Gideon bolted toward the wall. Chanting under his breath, he vaulted over the top stones, clearing them by a foot.

With a yelp, Finn flung himself backwards as the Amandán attacked. He found himself tumbling back down the slope, arms flailing as he tried to control his fall. Branches clawed at him, leaving burning scratches along his back and stomach where his tee shirt pulled up. The ground and sky exchanged places in slow motion.

Finn crashed to a halt at the bottom of the ravine, cracking his skull on a fallen log. For a moment, he lay breathless, the ground spinning as white-hot pain tore through his head. Stars flickered at the edge of his sight.

Feeling the vibration of massive feet thundering toward him, he rolled over with a groan, his eyes watering with pain. Struggling to rise, his fingers brushed against something cool and smooth and hard under a layer of leaves.

The knife.

Finn fumbled for the weapon. Lurching to his feet, he swayed, then braced himself for the assault. Bile burned his throat. He swallowed as the Amandán charged down the hill toward him. Branches snapped beneath its feet like broken bones. It ran skewed to one side, ape-like, on all fours. Finn locked his trembling knees and tightened his grip. For a moment, the goblin seemed to fill his vision. Every detail was enlarged, from the threads of slobber dangling from its yellow teeth to the twigs matted in its dirty green pelt. A rank stench filled the air—like someone's breath just after they've vomited. Into dirty socks.

"Drop, Finn!"

Even before he hit the ground, Gideon's blade flashed end over end past his head. With a moist *thwack* it buried itself hilt-deep in the creature.

Curled on his side, Finn squinted as ash blew everywhere, coating him and the surrounding vegetation. After a few moments, he opened his eyes, grimacing at the sour taste of leftover goblin on his lips. He flopped over. A warm trickle ran down the side of his face. Staring up at the branches overhead, the world darkened around him. Vaguely, he wondered at the sound of footsteps crashing through the underbrush. His eyelids fluttered closed for a moment.

A hand touched his shoulder. He blinked. Gideon was kneeling beside him, concern tightening his features. A second knife was ready in one fist. "Finn? Are ye with me, lad?"

"D-did we get it?" Finn whispered back. His eyes slid shut before his master could answer.

ight

Standing at Finn's bedroom window, Gideon gazed into the forest beyond the wall. The familiar anger tightened the muscles in his back and shoulders. It whispered in his head, urging him to strike out at anything. At anyone. He took a deep breath and relaxed the hands fisted by his sides. Glancing over a shoulder at the figure lying motionless on the bed, he frowned in surprise at the unexpected protectiveness that swept through him. He turned back to the window. "Come near mine again, beasties," he spoke to the empty woods, "be it me home or apprentice, and I'll—"

"G-eon?"

The Knight spun around at the slurred voice behind him. Hurrying over to the bed, he pulled the chair closer and took a seat. "And the hero awakes."

"My head hurts," Finn complained.

"Aye, no doubt. Since ye attacked a tree with it. The tree won, surprisingly, considering that thick noggin of yers."

"Ha, ha. Funny." Finn blinked as he looked around the bedroom. "How did I get here?"

"I carried ye." Gideon leaned over and pushed Finn's hair off his forehead. He examined the wound for a moment, then reached for the rag soaking in a bowl on the nightstand. A spicy, earthy aroma, like coffee mixed with peppermint, wafted up from the warm potion. Wringing the cloth out, he folded it into a small square and pressed it against Finn's injury.

Finn winced. "I like the way the *slainte* nettle smells, but man, that stuff stings like crazy!"

"Ah, ye whine like a wee babe. Here—hold this on for a bit longer." Gideon let go as Finn took over. After a few minutes, he took the cloth away. "Can ye sit up?" He waited until Finn pushed back against the headboard, then stuffed a pillow behind him.

Gideon picked up a steaming mug sitting next to the bowl and held it out. "Sip it slowly. T'will speed up the healing of both yer head wound and any bruises or scratches."

Cradling the cup in both hands, Finn sipped cautiously. He smacked his lips. "Tastes like you put honey in it."

"Aye—a bit of sweet. Some De Danaan do not enjoy its flavor."

"Not me! I could drink this stuff all day."

Gideon frowned when his apprentice took another gulp. "I wouldn't become too enamored with the brew. Too much *slainte* nettle tea can cause *problems* for our kind."

"Like what?"

"An excess of *slainte* nettle makes us inebriated."

"Inebriated?"

"Drunk."

Finn stared down into his mug. "Like how much excess?"

"Six or seven gallons, depending on the individual."

"Six or seven gallons! I'd be like a water balloon after drinking all that."

"Or ye'd be spending a great deal of time seeing a man about a horse."

Finn laughed at the old expression, one hand holding his bruised side. The corner of Gideon's mouth twitched as he took the mug before it spilled and set it back on the nightstand. Still chuckling, Finn leaned back against the pillow.

"So we got it, right? The Amandán?"

"Aye, we did. However..." He paused. *Should I tell him?*

"What's wrong? Did I lose the knife again?"

"No. All weapons are cleaned and accounted for. But I am concerned about—"

"Gideon, I'm sorry," Finn said in a rush. "Sorry I was acting like a jack-butt earlier. I know you want me to get better at controlling my temper."

The Knight raised a hand. "'Tis not that. Well, not exactly. Certainly, we will work on that temper of yers. What I want to discuss are these repeated attacks by the Amandán."

Finn's eyes widened. "You mean, this...this isn't normal?"

"Not at this magnitude." Gideon leaned back. "So, tell me. How much do ye know about the very beginnings of our race?"

"Just that the Tuatha De Danaan all started in Ireland. That we got kicked out by humans. And that the Amandán hate our guts. And vice versa." He glanced at Gideon. "I bet there's a lot more to it than that."

"Aye, there is. And if ye'll indulge me, I shall tell ye the tale in full." Stretching out his legs, Gideon settled himself more comfortably and began.

"Since the beginning of time, the non-human beings of Ireland, the Tuatha De Danaan and the Amandán, have battled for control of our beloved land. For both have a claim to it, as our ancestral home. In fact, the Amandán believe they first emerged from the peat bogs of Eire—the Bog-born. In a sense, they and the land are one."

"What about us?"

"Why, we are descendents of Danu, one of the Celtic goddesses of war. Hence our *flair* for battle. She bestowed upon us the Emerald Isle as our own as long as we could hold it from the Amandán, and our struggle with the beasties would have been contained to Ireland if it wasn't for the invaders."

"The Bronze Age humans?"

"Aye. And at first, we welcomed the mortals. Their bronze weapons were more lethal than our flint ones. Allied with them, we were able to drive out most of the Amandán. Because of that, the Amandán have even more reason to hate the De Danaan with a deep and lasting fury. But, once the threat from the goblins was no more, the mortals, who by that time outnumbered us by the thousands, turned on us."

"But we're so much like humans. Why did they want to get rid of us?"

"Fear. Fear of creatures that were different. So, they decided to rid Ireland of all such beings. Our ancestors, along with the Amandán, were scattered to the four corners of the world. But the war between us and the beasties continues. Just more clandestinely."

"Clandestinely? What does that mean?"

"Secretly," Gideon explained. "Can ye imagine what would happen if humans really knew about us? Why, we would turn from being hunters to being hunted! Fortunately, the Amandán still fear them. Somewhat."

"How did so many of them end up *here?*" Finn picked up the mug and took another sip as he listened.

"The beasties are earth-dwellers—they gain strength from it. They migrated to lands with abandoned mines."

"Like Colorado."

"And other places. For example, Pennsylvania is densely populated with the beasties. The old coal mines back East have some of the most vicious tribes of Amandán."

"And bronze only weakens the Amandán, it doesn't kill them. But *we* can die from any weapon, right?"

The Knight nodded. "Whatever kills a mortal can kill us. Except our powers and our training make us just a wee bit more difficult to destroy. Always remember this, Finn." He tapped his torc for emphasis. "In spite of being part human, ye come from an ancient line of warriors."

Finn studied the Knight's gold collar. "How old were you when you fought your first Amandán one-on-one?"

"Oh, 'tis certain I was much, *much* older than ye before I earned this. No need to rush, boyo. There are more than enough goblins. I'll be sure to save one for ye."

"Okay." Finn smiled, and then asked, "So, is there anything that can actually *kill* an Amandán?"

"I only know of one weapon. A mythical one at that. The Spear of the Tuatha De Danaan."

"Who has it? Where is it?"

"Oh, it's been lost for centuries upon centuries. If it ever really existed. Supposedly, it can only be wielded by a De Danaan, and its touch is deadly to the Amandán. The beasties have always feared it might found again. Ironically, it is also called—" Gideon paused at the sound of his apprentice's stomach growling.

"I think I'm feeling better now." Finn swung his legs off the bed. He started to rise when Gideon put out a hand.

"Oh, no, ye don't, boyo. Ye're to take it easy for the rest of the afternoon. I'll bring ye a tray. And then we'll finish our chat."

Settling back, Finn clasped his hands behind his head. "You know, I could get used to this. How about breakfast in bed tomorrow?"

"Not bleedin' likely," the Knight murmured as he stood and left the room.

ine

Humming under his breath, Gideon selected a pear from the basket on the counter and added it to the luncheon tray before heading out of the kitchen and across the living room. As he reached the foot of the stairs, a heavy blow rattled the front door, followed by a second one.

"Ye gods, he's going to knock me house down one day," Gideon muttered good-humoredly. He walked over and rested the tray across the wooden crate. He smiled as he opened the door.

"Mac Roth," he said to the bearded man standing on the porch. "*Fáilte*." Gideon clasped the man's forearm in greeting, then ushered him inside.

"A fine day to ye, Lir." The man ducked as he entered, his wild mane of red hair a scant inch from the ceiling. A head taller than Gideon, his bulk filled the small space as he glanced down at the tray. "Am I interrupting yer lunch, now?" He shrugged out of his leather jacket and tossed it over one of the coat hooks. A thick chest and shoulders strained the seams of a faded sweatshirt emblazoned with the slogan "Fighting Irish Is Redundant".

"No, not at all. I've a battered apprentice upstairs."

"Apparently." Mac Roth nodded toward the dried bloodstain on the sleeve of Gideon's denim shirt. "And how is young Finnegan?"

"Come, and I'll introduce ye." Gideon picked up the tray and led the way upstairs. "The lad's been with me for scarcely a week, and he's already had two engagements with the Amandán."

"Why, then it's true." Mac Roth followed, the steps protesting at his bulk.

"What's true?"

"The rising number of attacks along the eastern side of the Rockies, especially here in High Springs."

"Does anyone know why?"

"Iona has a theory—"

"That sorceress," Gideon scoffed over a shoulder.

"Sorceress she may be, but she knows as much about the Amandán as any of us."

"All she'll do is confound us with vague prophecies from those ancient texts of hers, and then step aside as we De Danaan battle for our lives."

"Still bitter, eh, Lir? Why, I thought ye would have let go of yer anger and grief after all these years."

"Would ye?" He nudged Finn's door open with his knee and stepped inside, Mac Roth at his heels. They stopped talking when they noticed Finn sitting cross-legged on the bed.

"Mac Roth, meet Finnegan MacCullen," Gideon said. He walked around the bed and handed the tray to the boy. "Finn, this is me oldest and finest friend, Knight Mac Roth. We've known each other since we were both apprentices back in Ireland."

Finn looked up wide-eyed as the other De Danaan approached. "Uh … hello." He nodded once. "And *fáilte*," he added, after a subtle throat-clearing from Gideon.

Mac Roth grinned, his teeth flashing white inside his fiery beard. "Fergus MacCullen's son. Why, I knew yer father. A formidable warrior. And I had met yer mother, Molly Rose MacCullen, once. She was a rare beauty." Sticking out a hand, his blue eyes twinkled as he waited until the apprentice clasped his meaty forearm in the traditional greeting. Squeezing Finn's, he added, "Ye've a strong arm, lad. Gideon must be feeding ye well." Letting go, he took the chair Gideon offered and sank down. He gestured toward the food. "I'll talk while ye eat." He waited until Gideon perched on the edge of the bed. "As I was saying, other De Danaan are reporting more and more encounters with the Amandán. The beasties are becoming bolder."

"Ye said Iona had a theory as to why?" Gideon reminded him.

Mac Roth leaned back in the chair, the legs creaking alarmingly. "Aye—the Spear."

"You mean the Spear of Tuatha De Danaan? We were just talking about it." Finn asked around his sandwich.

"The very one." Mac Roth reached over and snagged a carrot off Finn's plate, munching it down in two bites. "It is also known as Gideon's Spear—" He started to add more when Finn interrupted him.

"Why didn't you tell me it had another name?" He looked at Gideon. "*Your* name?"

"I was about to inform ye of all this when we got sidetracked by yer stomach. And stop bleedin' interrupting."

"Iona has heard a rumor," continued Mac Roth, hiding a grin in his beard, "that the Spear may be here. In High Springs. Hidden somewhere amongst the De Danaan. She also believes that the Amandán know of this rumor and are attempting to kill as many of us as they can before we locate the weapon and use it against them."

Gideon sighed. "And since there are so few of us, the Amandán might prevail this time."

Finn frowned for a moment, then brightened. "Hey! Maybe humans might be willing to help us again. Like in the old days. I mean, if we told them what was really going on."

Gideon snorted. "Let me play that scenario for ye, Finn." He gave a nod as he pretended to speak with someone in the corner. "Why, top of the day to ye, Mr. and Mrs. Twenty-first Century Human. We've never met, but I'm Gideon Lir. A Knight of the Tuatha De

Danaan—what ye might call Fey or Fairy. No. No wings. I *do* use magic and medieval weapons to battle goblin-like creatures with nasty dispositions and terrible body odor. Say, would ye care to help? I've a spare hunting knife and... Wait! Do not run away. To be sure, I am quite harmless!"

As Finn laughed, trying not to choke on his lunch, Mac Roth flung his head back and roared. Gasping for breath, they applauded Gideon, who rose, placed a hand on his chest, and took a bow.

"And that, me lad," he added, "is why we don't tell mortals. Best to keep our identity secret."

Still chuckling, Mac Roth stood up. "Now, ye two are closest to the mountains, and the old mining district, so be wary." Pausing at the door, he glanced over his shoulder. "Finn, I've an apprentice about yer age—Asher O'Neill." He looked at Gideon. "What do ye say we take these two hunting soon, eh?"

"Name the place and time and we'll be there," replied the Knight.

"How about a night hunt by the river? Where it runs along the edge of the city. Say, in a couple of weeks?"

"So, ye've gotten over yer fear of the dark, have ye?" Gideon said with a straight face.

"Aye. About the same time ye learned which end of yer weapon to use." The Knights both laughed, then Mac Roth waved good-bye. "I'll see meself out."

They sat listening to his heavy tread, then the thud of the front door closing. After a moment, a vehicle roared to life, the growl fading as he drove away. Gideon walked over to the window. *Strange, that after all these years, talk of the Spear is surfacing again. But Mac Roth is mad to think I'll ever trust Iona, much less listen to her.* The voice of his apprentice brought him back from his thoughts.

"Gideon? Do you think the Amandán are out there right now? Hunting *us*?"

"I do."

"So what do we do? To protect ourselves?"

The Knight pulled out his knife and ran a thumb along the blade, then held it up to the light. He glanced back over his shoulder and smiled grimly. "Why, we hunt them back."

Ten

The Journal of Finnegan MacCullen: June 15

It seems like all we've done these last two weeks is eat, sleep, train, and do chores. Not always in that order.

Gideon said he's never run into so many Amandán. Even though we're not looking for them. That's because they're looking for us. Waiting for us to let our guard down.

We're going hunting tonight with Knight Mac Roth and his apprentice. I hope I don't screw up in front of everyone.

What I Learned ~~Today~~ Lately:

I found out more about the Spear. It is somehow connected to mortals. According to the legend, after the humans broke their alliance with us, a mortal and a De Danaan who had remained friends decided to make the Spear together. They intended it to be the ultimate weapon against the Amandán. No one knows who the mortal was, but the De Danaan was this gifted blacksmith named Gideon Black Hand. That's why we sometimes call it Gideon's Spear. The problem is, we don't know where it is anymore.

"Is that them?" Finn asked, peering through the truck's windshield across the almost deserted parking lot. An old Jeep with a crumpled fender waited in the light of the single streetlamp. As he watched, a massive figure stepped around the back end of the vehicle and waved them over. A shorter figure followed.

Gideon wheeled the truck around and pulled to a stop, the brakes grinding. As the engine died with a grateful sigh, he turned and fixed Finn with a stern eye. "Remember, ye and Asher are to watch and learn. Stay where we tell ye. Do what we tell ye. Or I'll tan yer backside."

"Okay already. You told me that like a hundred..." Finn stopped and swallowed the rest of the sentence at his master's expression. "I mean, yes, sir." He waited until Gideon stepped out of the truck before rolling his eyes. He hopped out, shoved the door closed with his shoulder, and joined the trio standing between the two vehicles.

Mac Roth gestured toward the sandy-haired boy next to him. Finn noted that the boy was about his height and had the same compact build. "Finn, this is my apprentice, Asher O'Neill. Asher, meet Finnegan MacCullen."

"Hi, Asher." Finn put out his hand like Gideon had coached him and waited.

"How's it going?" Asher nodded once in greeting, his eyes the ancient De Danaan blue. He hesitated for a moment before shaking hands with Finn.

"Right. Now, for the hunt." Mac Roth turned and led the way out of the parking lot to the trailhead. Their feet crunched on the gravel path as they walked in single file down a gentle slope. The river at the bottom gleamed with a silvery sheen.

Reaching the sandy bank, they stopped and gazed first upstream, then down. Thick willows lined both sides of the shallow river, scarcely more than a creek, while boulders squatted here and there, their shadows inky pools from the light of the full moon. As the Knights stepped away to confer in private, Finn turned to the other boy.

"So, how long have you been Mac Roth's apprentice?"

"About four months," Asher replied curtly. He pulled out his knife and flipped it into the air. The bronze winked in the moonlight. He caught it by the handle with ease.

"Lucky you! I've been with Gideon for only—"

"Look," Asher interrupted him, keeping his voice low. "I'm here to learn how to hunt. Not make friends with a halfer."

"W-what did you call me?"

"Halfer. Mac Roth told me about you. About your mother." Asher examined the edge of his blade, then stared at Finn with cold eyes. "So, make sure you stay out of my way. Got it? I don't want to miss my chance at earning my torc just because a wannabe De Danaan screws up the hunt."

For a moment, Finn's mouth hung open. His cheeks burned with humiliation. Then anger. Before he could move or say a word, Gideon gave a sharp whistle.

"Front and center, boyos," he called. Asher sneered at Finn standing frozen, then turned and hurried toward the Knights. "Move yer arse, Finn," Gideon barked.

Seething with anger, Finn walked stiff-legged over to the rest. His pulse humming in his ears, he nodded without listening to Gideon's instructions. *What an ass*, he thought. *Asher the Ass.* His lips twitched at a sudden thought. *No. Wait. It's* Ass-her. He jumped when Gideon snapped at him.

"I said, do ye understand me?"

Finn blinked and looked up at him. "Y-yes, sir." Before Gideon could question him further, he followed Asher over to a massive boulder, the top of it higher than his head, and took a stance in the protection of the rock. He stood as far away from the other boy as he could.

"Asher O'Neill," called Mac Roth as he pulled a knife and a hatchet from his belt, "Move from that spot and ye'll feel the back of me hand." Without another word, he plunged into the undergrowth.

"And the same to ye, Finn," Gideon added, his favorite knife already in his hand. He turned and followed in Mac Roth's wake. The vegetation slapped back behind them. A further rustle, then silence.

For few minutes, Finn stood staring at the spot where the Knights had disappeared; he pointedly ignored the other apprentice. The river rippled and splashed as the night air cooled the heat in his face. *Just great,* he grumbled to himself. *How am I supposed to learn to hunt just standing around? Especially with this jerk.*

He pulled out his knife and slouched against the rock. Using the point of the weapon, he idly picked at the lichen covering the rock like a case of bad acne. He flicked a piece away. Into Asher's face.

Totally unintentional, of course.

"Hey! Knock it off!"

"Make me." Finn threw a larger piece at him. "*Ass-her.*"

Asher narrowed his eyes. Glancing around, he spied a weathered branch the same length as his knife. He picked it up. "Halfer," he spat back, and pitched the stick with a sideways, boomerang-y throw.

Finn twisted to one side. He watched as the stick sailed past him and fell with a splash into the river. He glanced back in time to see Asher snatch up a fist-sized rock.

Shifting the knife to his left hand, Finn hastily scooped his own rock out of the sand. He held it at shoulder-height, his arm cocked back. They stood a few yards apart, eyes locked on each other and poised for battle. The river seemed to laugh at them as it gurgled along.

Then, the quiet of the night exploded.

"*FAUGH A BALLAGH!*"

Shouting the Irish war cry, Gideon burst out of the bushes a dozen yards downstream. He sprinted toward them. Without slowing, he flung a taunting challenge over his shoulder. In hot pursuit, a second shape crashed through the willows. Snarling like a pissed-off pit bull, the Amandán churned up sand and mud as it ran, its dangling arms almost touching the ground. It sped up and closed the gap between itself and the Knight.

Finn's heart flew into his throat. He watched as his master leaped on top of a goblin-high boulder nearby and took a defensive stance. Balancing easily on the rock, the Knight raised his weapon aloft. Moonlight danced along the blade. It flashed above Gideon's head like a flame.

Then he heard his master laugh. "Come closer, ye manky beast," he shouted when the Amandán skidded to a halt at the foot of the stone. "I dinna' sharpen this blade for nothing."

The goblin stretched to full height. With surprising speed, it swiped at Gideon's ankle, managing to snag the hem of his jeans with black-tipped fingers. It bared its teeth in triumph.

Without thinking, Finn threw the rock in his hand as hard as he could; it bounced off the Amandán's head with a dull *thunk*. The goblin yelped, let go of Gideon's jeans, and whirled around. "*Nar,* one of the whelps."

When ye can, take the fight to yer enemy. His master's voice seemed to speak in his head. *Control the field of battle. A timely attack has won many a war.*

Finn's voice cracked as he let out a yell and charged.

And tripped over a half-buried log in the sand.

He slammed face-first into the ground, sand abrading his cheek. The air whooshed out of him. He laid there, mouth opening and shutting like a stranded fish. His lungs seemed to have forgotten how to operate. Dimly, he heard Gideon and Mac Roth shouting, one in anger and one in triumph. Suddenly, the shriek of the goblin pierced the night, then was cut short.

Just as Finn's lungs decided to get back to work, a pair of hands grabbed him and yanked him to his feet. The blade fell from his grasp as he was spun around.

Gideon clutched his shoulders, his grip like iron and his eyes ablaze. Finn could almost feel the heatwaves of anger coming off his master. "What, in the name of all the gods, do ye think ye're doing?" He shook Finn roughly. "I ordered ye to stay by the bleedin' rock!"

"But I—" croaked Finn, then stopped when Gideon yelled again.

"The beast could have turned on ye! Before I could have reached ye!"

"But I—" His teeth clattered together when his master shook him again.

A massive shape loomed up next to them. "Now, Lir," Mac Roth said, laying a massive paw on his friend's shoulder. "Go easy on the lad. Why, Finn was only doing what any apprentice should do."

"Get himself killed before his fourteenth birthday?"

"No, ye thick-headed bog trotter." Unmoved by Gideon's anger, he calmly wiped his hatchet with a rag. "Protect his master's back on the hunt."

Gideon's mouth tightened as he glared at Finn. The muscles in his jaw jumped. Without another word, he whirled around and stomped off, slashing at the tips of the innocent willow branches with his blade.

Finn stood in shock, heart hammering against his ribs. For some reason, tears prickled his eyelids. He bent over and picked up his knife, then dragged a sleeve across his eyes. He glanced over at Mac Roth, mortified.

The Knight pretended not to notice. "Ye gods, but Lir can scream like a banshee, eh, lad?" He gave Finn a wink.

Finn sniffed and chuckled. "Aye, that he can," he said, mimicking the Knight's accent.

Mac Roth patted his shoulder. "T'will be all right." With a nod, he turned around and headed back up the slope, Asher trailing behind him.

Finn let out a long breath. He wiped the knife clean of sand before tucking it away. A few yards upstream, Gideon whirled around and started back toward him, anger still plain in his stiff walk. Finn fought the desire to back away when his master drew even with him.

"Truck. Now." Gideon stabbed a finger toward the path.

They were silent all the way home.

The Journal of Gideon Lir: June 16

We hunted with Mac Roth and young Asher last night. Only one goblin accounted for. I certainly wish we could do more than just slow them down. Mac Roth and I both believe we are fighting a losing battle. There are simply too many of them.

As Mac Roth so bluntly put it this evening, "They breed like rabbits." Except he used another word for *breeding*. I had to remind him that there were young ears nearby.

My old friend then reminded *me* that those 'young ears' were thirteen-year-old boys, and they already know all about the rabbit-breeding thing. At least in theory.

Poor Finn. I lost my temper with him after he disobeyed me. I hauled him over the coals quite severely in front of the others.

Better for him to be embarrassed than dead.

Eleven

The next morning, Finn swallowed as he tugged at the hem of his tee shirt. Stalling for time, he pressed his fingers against the stone in his pocket for courage, then forced himself to step into the kitchen. He hesitated when he spied his master at the table writing in his journal, steam rising from the morning mug of tea at his elbow.

"Uh—'morning, Gideon."

The Knight grunted in response. He paused to turn the page before resuming his task. A rock-heavy silence followed; the scratching of the pen filled the room. Finn cleared his throat and tried again.

"Sorry about last night."

Gideon threw the pen down and twisted around, hooking an arm over the back of the chair. He stared at Finn, eyes blue ice. "Disobey me again, Finnegan MacCullen, and the Amandán will be the least of yer worries. Understand?"

"Yes, sir."

Gideon rose and walked over. "Because if I lose ye to those monsters, 'twill not be due to the stupidity ye demonstrated last night." He cuffed Finn affectionately. "Now, be a good lad, and go fetch the newspaper."

"Yes, sir." With a lighter heart, Finn turned and hurried through the house. Easing out the front door, he walked down the steps and along the path, leaving the gate ajar. As he reached the sidewalk, he heard a low rumbling. He squinted into the morning sun and stared at the house across the street.

A lanky boy about his age trudged down its driveway, rolling a large, plastic garbage container behind him. Wheeling it into place along the curb, he glanced up and noticed Finn.

"Hey. How's it going?" He secured the lid with a thump of his fist.

"Um, okay." Finn noticed the newspaper lying in the street. He walked over and picked it up.

"Did you just move here?" the boy asked as Finn hesitated in the middle of the road.

"Yeah. Well, *I* did. About three weeks ago. Gideon has lived here for a long time. He's my new guardian," Finn said. *Good thing Gideon and I came up with that cover story,* he thought. *Just in case.*

"Cool!" The boy grinned. "It'll be nice to have another guy around. I'm Rafe Steel."

"Finn MacCullen."

"Like a fish?"

Like a fish? he thought. "Oh, I get it. No, Finn's short for Finnegan."

Rafe's black eyes grew wide. "I can see why you go by Finn," he said, then winced. "Sorry. I shouldn't have said that."

Finn laughed. "It's okay."

"Hey, doofus! You forgot this." A girl, a few inches shorter and with Rafe's lanky build and ebony skin, walked toward them, her shoulder-length black curls pulled back with a headband. She carried an empty pizza box in one hand. Flipping open the container, she tossed it in. "Hi," she said, noticing Finn for the first time.

"Uh, this is my little sister, Savannah. Savannah, this is Finn MacCullen. He just moved here."

"Hey, Finn." She smiled, the dimples in her cheeks matching her brother's. "And I've told you to stop introducing me as your *little* sister," she added as she punched Rafe in the arm. "You've got like, what, six minutes on me?"

"Let me guess—twins?" Finn looked from one to the other.

"Yeah. Twins." Rafe made a face. "Why couldn't she have been a brother?"

Finn grinned at Savannah's chuff of exasperation. "So, why haven't I seen you two around before?"

"Oh, we go to South Africa every year for a few weeks. As soon as school's out. To visit our grandfather," Savannah said. "We just got back yesterday evening. In fact, we're still unpacking our—"

"Finnegan?"

All three looked over as Gideon strolled across the yard toward them. Pausing at the end of the path, he nodded politely at the Steel children.

"Good morning." He opened the gate wider. "Come, lad," he called.

Finn's face burned at his master's tone. And choice of words. *Dude, I'm not a dog!* "I've gotta go."

Rafe grinned in understanding. "Later, Finn." He waved a hand and headed up the driveway, his sister on his heels.

Finn whirled around. "Why did you have to embarrass me like that?" he grumbled as he stomped home and handed the paper over. "I was just talking to them." He yanked the gate shut with a clang before following his master up the porch steps.

"Well, I'd rather ye not," Gideon said over his shoulder. "Relationships with mortals cause nothing but complications for our kind." He opened the screen and went in.

Finn paused, one foot on the lowest step. He glanced back across the street. "Says you."

Twelve

Pulling the bronze wire tight, Finn wrapped another strand around the gatepost, then twisted the ends together with a pair of pliers. The reddish metal twined around the bars like the stripes on a candy cane. *This should slow the Amandán down.* Taking a break, he gave a nod of satisfaction as he straightened up and pulled his sweaty tee away from his body.

"What's all that for?"

He spun around. Rafe was walking toward him holding a soda pop can in one hand. Reaching behind, Finn yanked his shirt down over his sheathed knife.

"Just something to keep out…you know, animals." He grinned, pleased to see the other boy again after only a few days.

Rafe took a sip, then nodded. "Mom tried aluminum foil once, but the rabbits still did a smackdown on her geraniums." He ran a finger along the wire. "Is this copper?"

"Bronze." Finn wiped his face on a sleeve.

"Here." Rafe held out the can. "Want some?"

"Oh, thanks." Finn drank gratefully, then handed it back. They both laughed when he burped. "Sorry."

"You should be. That was totally lame. Here, listen to this." Rafe chugged the rest of the can, then let loose a drawn-out rumble.

They laughed again, Rafe pinching his nose to keep soda from spraying. As the boy held his arm up, Finn's eyes widened with curiosity.

"Hey, what's that?"

"What—this?" A slender bracelet, woven of coarse black hairs intermingled with tawny ones, encircled Rafe's wrist. The ends were tied together with leather thongs. "Oh, this is from a ceremony I did with my grandfather. In South Africa. It's made from real lion's hair. From the tip of its tail."

Finn peered more closely. "What kind of ceremony?"

"Like an initiation. First step into manhood, and all that. They used to have the teenage boys of the tribe kill a real lion to demonstrate their bravery. Nowadays, we just spend the night in the bush by ourselves with nothing but a campfire and a spear. Grandfather said it was still a test of bravery. So, I did this summer while I was there. And he gave me this afterwards."

Like the torc we earn when we bag our first Amandán, Finn thought. "Was it scary? Or just boring?"

Rafe hesitated for a moment. "Okay, don't laugh, but I almost pissed myself when a herd of antelope wandered by in the middle of the night. They were making all this noise in the bush on their way to the watering hole. I couldn't see them. All I heard was this loud breathing and snorting and branches breaking." He fingered the bracelet. "But I stuck it out. I must have fallen asleep under that tree, because the next thing I knew, it was getting lighter and birds were squawking. And then I watched the sun rise over the savanna." He looked up at Finn. "It made me feel..." His voice trailed off.

"Made you feel like you were part of something. Something really old, but really powerful."

"Yeah."

They looked at each other. An unspoken recognition passed between them. With a grin, Rafe gestured toward his house.

"Hey, do you want to see my African stuff? I got to bring back the spear and even a shield." He snorted. "After we filled out about a million forms and promised not to hijack the plane with them."

Finn glanced at his empty driveway. *Gideon won't be back for awhile,* he thought. *I'll just stay a few minutes.* "Sure. But then, I've got to finish up here." Leaving the pliers and the coil of wire by the gate, Finn followed Rafe across the street.

The boys hurried up the walk toward the tall brick house and through its front door. Finn eyed the stylish foyer, complete with an antique entryway table and gleaming marble floor. *It's sure fancier than ours. Must be nice to have a lot of money.*

"Rafe?" called a woman's voice. A tall, dark-skinned woman, her face elegant with high cheekbones, appeared. She pulled on a white lab coat as she approached, heels clicking in a rapid staccato. "I'm needed at the hospital and your father ran to the hardware store, so I want you to—" She stopped, noticing Finn.

"Mom, this is Finn MacCullen. He moved here while we were gone. I was going to show him the stuff I brought back."

"Hello, Finn. I'm Susanna Steel," Mrs. Steel introduced herself, her smile warm. "Welcome to the neighborhood. Rafe will be thrilled to have another boy around." She picked up her purse from the table and began rummaging for car keys. "Which house is yours?"

"The small green one with the stone wall around it. Kind of across from here."

Mrs. Steel paused in her search. "Gideon Lir's house?" A faint line appeared between her eyebrows.

Finn nodded. "He's my guardian. Do you know him?"

"We've spoken a few times." She studied him intently for a moment, then her face relaxed. "And how do you like Colorado, so far?"

"Oh, I'm from Denver. I used to live with my aunt and uncle up there." Finn shifted from foot to foot. An odd reluctance to give more details crept over him.

"Would you mind me asking what happened to your parents?"

"They died when I was five. In a hunting accident."

"Oh, I'm sorry, Finn." Mrs. Steel tilted her head to one side. "And so, now you live with Mr. Lir? Not your aunt and uncle anymore?"

"Mom!" Rafe rolled his eyes. "What's with the third degree?"

"No, it's okay." Finn glanced over at Rafe, then back to his mom. "Um, Gideon is an old friend of our family. Plus, my aunt and uncle have nine other kids, so this just worked out better. And I am learning a ton of stuff from him." Finn grinned. *Stuff like how to peg a monster between the eyes with a hunting knife.*

Mrs. Steel smiled back. Glancing at her watch, she sighed. "Okay, I'm off. Rafe, fifteen minutes with Finn, then you need to get the backyard mowed and your bag unpacked. Your dad will be back shortly. Finn, I hope to see you again soon." She hurried out the door.

Rafe shook his head. "Now that we're through the security check with Dr. Steel, I'll show you my spear." He led the way along the hall and up a curving flight of stairs. Reaching the top, they hooked a right into the first bedroom. Rafe shoved a partially unpacked duffle bag out of their way.

"That's it." He pointed at the spear resting on the desk. Nearby, an oval shield, a little shorter than the boys, leaned against the wall. Rafe rapped his knuckles against the black and white hardened cow leather. "My dad went to get some hooks so I can hang them on the wall."

Finn picked up the spear. The thick wooden handle was decorated with bands of ornamental beads in crayon-bright colors. A broad, leaf-shaped blade was attached to the business end.

"It's more for stabbing than throwing. That's why it's shorter than a regular spear," Rafe explained. "Real ones wouldn't have all that decoration. The handles would be plain."

Finn thrust it in the air a few times. "Nice balance. Is it bronze?"

"Yeah. For some reason, my grandfather wanted me to have a bronze one instead of iron."

As Finn laid it back down, he noticed a small telescope next to the window. "Is that yours?"

"Yeah. Well, my dad's and mine—he's a science teacher at the high school. There's going to be an eclipse of the sun on July tenth and I thought I might get a special filter for this so I can watch without hurting my eyes. Of course, this event is only a partial, not an annular eclipse, which is more rare and..." He paused, and shot Finn a glance. "I know what you're thinking," he said with a self-conscious expression.

Finn frowned in confusion. "What?"

"Well, that I'm some kind of science geek."

"What's wrong with being interested in—" Finn stopped when a light flickered through the window and bounced against the far wall. He bent over and peered out as his master's truck pulled into the driveway, the sun reflecting off its cracked windshield. "Gideon's back. I better get home." Sprinting out of the room, Finn pounded down the stairs, Rafe on his heels.

"Is he going to get mad because you didn't finish the gate?" Rafe asked as he ran ahead and opened the front door. He held it wide as Finn bolted through it.

"Oh, yeah!" *And for other reasons.* "I'll see you around," he yelled over his shoulder.

Running across the street, he slowed in relief at the sight of the empty truck cab. *He must have gone inside already*, Finn thought, halting by the gate. Panting, he crouched down on the sidewalk and uncoiled a section of wire, the metal hot from the sun. *Okay, look busy.* He measured another length. As he reached for the wire cutters, a shadow fell across him.

Thirteen

Finn froze as bare knuckles rapped on his skull. *This is* so *not good*, he thought.

"Hmm, I hear nary an echo, so I'm going to assume ye've a brain in there." Gideon stepped around him. "A brain that can follow simple directions. Directions such as, 'finish this gate by noon. And do not fraternize with the humans next door.'"

"I *am* almost finished." Finn rose to his feet and locked eyes with his master. "And anyway, they don't live *next door*. They live across the street. And kind of over to the left. Totally different."

Gideon's brows drew together. "I'll not have ye splitting hairs when I give ye an order to—"

At that moment, a dark form flew over them, stroking the air with its black wings. The crow cawed twice and disappeared behind the house as it sped toward the western hills.

Argument abandoned, Gideon whirled around and dashed along the side of the house, Finn on his heels. Together they ran across the backyard. Without breaking stride, the Knight pulled his knife out.

"Yer blade at the ready," he ordered, then came to a halt as Finn slowed, fumbling behind him for his weapon. "And ye're holding the bleedin' thing wrong!" He jerked the weapon away and spun it around. "*Handle* forward, *blade* back, until ye go into battle," he snapped, thrusting it back into the boy's hand.

"Yes, sir." Finn's cheeks reddened as he tightened his grip. His sweat made the leather grip slippery.

Chanting the Song in low voices, they picked up speed again and ran toward the wall. Gideon leaped first, his foot lightly pushing off the top stones. Finn followed with a one-handed vault. He landed next to Gideon on a path running along the rim of the ravine.

In a steady jog, they followed the trail north for a few minutes before turning and plunging down one side of the ravine and up the other. They struck another hiking path winding westward through the woods. Bushy scrub oaks, mixed with the occasional pine tree, formed screens on either side of the trail.

They headed deeper into the woods. Finn glanced around him at every crunch of last year's leaves and dead twigs. After a mile, Gideon halted and motioned for him to stop. The Knight cocked his head as he listened.

Finn peered up, craning his neck to search the cloudless sky, squinting into the midday sun. "There!" he cried, pointing toward the top of the next hill. A black X circled over a stand of pine trees.

Gideon ran a few steps, keeping his eyes locked on the crow. "Quickly, before it ..." He faltered, cursing under his breath as two more birds joined the first one.

"What's wrong?" Finn asked.

"Not a lone one. There's at least three Amandán." Gideon turned and studied Finn for a moment, then shook his head and slid his weapon back into its sheath. "We best leave them for another day."

Finn set his feet, a stubborn glint in his eyes. "Gideon, I can do this. I know I can." He smiled crookedly. "I'll even let you have two for yourself."

"Oh, ye will, will ye?" He pulled out the knife again, examining the blade as he pondered. "Cocky little git."

"Please, Gideon? I'll do dishes all week. Every meal."

"Ye already do dishes after every meal."

"Yeah, but I won't *complain* about it. I promise."

The Knight gazed up at the crows still soaring in a three-way dance over the tree tops, then looked over at Finn.

Finn raised his chin and stared back. He stood as tall as he could and threw back his shoulders, trying to make himself look bigger.

Gideon quirked an eyebrow. "'I am a bull of seven battles,' eh?"

"You got that right. I mean, yes, sir."

Without another word, they raced, side by side, after the birds.

His lungs burning, Finn wheezed for breath, stumbling backwards over a tree root as the Amandán lunged for him again. He hit the trunk of the massive Ponderosa pine with a shoulder and almost dropped the knife clutched in his hand. Sweat dripping down his face stung his eyes. He pressed his back against the rough bark, and sucked in another desperate breath. The stink of Amandán filled his nostrils and coated his tongue. With a silent curse, he stabbed at the goblin.

"Getting weary, little De Danaan?" it rasped in a mocking tone, as it scampered from side to side, trying to break through Finn's defenses.

"Don't let it flank ye," Gideon warned, fighting nearby. His clothes were already dusted with the ashy remains of the first Amandán. With blinding speed, he feinted and parried, his blade a blur as the second goblin rushed at him. He drove off the beast and edged closer to Finn. "Keep yer knife up and moving."

"'Kay," Finn gasped through a parched mouth. Long shadows stretched around them as the afternoon sun crept closer to the mountain tops. The muscles in his arms and legs screamed as he swung the knife at the Amandán. The goblin scrambled out of range, hooting in derision. Tears of frustration and exhaustion blurred Finn's vision. With a half-groan, half-sob, he crumpled to one knee.

"Oh, no, ye don't!" Gideon leaped to Finn's side. He reached down and grabbed him by the back of his shirt with one hand, hauling him upright. "On yer feet, boyo. The ground is no place for a warrior."

They pressed further back against the tree, eyeing the Amandán huddled together a few yards away, speaking to each other in an undertone. Finn swiped at his grimy face, grateful the sweat camouflaged the few tears that had fallen. He looked up wearily as his master nudged him.

"'Tis a pleasant day for a hunt, to be sure. But I dinna think it would go on this long." Gideon smiled grimly, his black hair salted with ash. His face was streaked with goblin residue and sweat. He licked dry lips, then made a face at the taste and spat, one eye on the goblins. "And what would they be planning?"

"Gives us the runt for our supper," one of the goblins suddenly growled at the Knight. "And we lets ye live."

"Why, he wouldn't be more than a mouthful. The boyo is naught but skin and bones," Gideon pointed out. "I've a better barter. Ye leave now and I swear I'll not kill ye." He paused, then amended. "Until later." In spite of his weariness, Finn snorted with laughter.

"*Nar*, what kinds of barter is that?"

"The Tuatha De Danaan kind."

The Amandán glanced at each other, then charged. Standing shoulder to shoulder, master and apprentice slashed and stabbed, Gideon making two thrusts for each one of Finn's. Gasping the Song between frantic gulps of air, Finn noticed Gideon chanting along with him. His clear tenor was supported by his master's deeper, richer baritone.

Suddenly, a rush of energy surged through him, the blending of their voices giving him a second wind. As they sang, Gideon gestured with his knife. Finn nodded. Tightening his grip, he blinked the sweat from his eyes and took a deep breath.

"*Faugh a ballagh!*" they shouted in unison, and sprang forward. Surprised at the De Danaan's fierce charge, the Amandán tripped over each other as they scrambled to flee. Too late.

Ash flew everywhere as the beasts exploded.

After drying his hair until he resembled a redheaded hedgehog, Finn wiped his neck and chest, then tossed the towel over the shower curtain rod. The minty-sweet fragrance of shampoo filled the bathroom. *Hope I got it all—leftover Amandán is tough to wash out*, he thought, smoothing his mop. *I see why Gideon wears his so short—maybe I should get mine cut.* He pinned his hair flat with both hands and stared in the mirror. "Nah, I don't think so." Grabbing a clean tee shirt off the counter, he pulled it on as Gideon called from downstairs.

"Finn? Supper's ready. And bring yer dirty clothes with ye."

Loping down the stairs, filthy jeans and tee wadded under one arm, Finn hurried through the house, pausing to toss the clothes onto the floor of the tiny laundry-half bath combo just off the kitchen. He closed his eyes and inhaled the aroma of hot grilled-cheese sandwiches as he slid into his place at the table.

"Ye gods, I'm starving. I didn't get lunch because—" He froze. His jaw dropped as he looked down. A thin crescent of gold rested on his empty plate. "Oh. Oh, wow," he whispered, staring at the newly polished torc.

Gideon turned from the sink, drying his hands. "Bring it here, and I'll put it on ye."

With unsteady fingers, Finn reached out and picked it up. The overhead light glinted off the twisted wires forming the curved band. The two ends were finished with hammered orbs of golden metal. *It's not as heavy as I thought it would be*, he thought as he rose to his feet and carried it over. It felt cool against his palms, still warm from the shower.

The Knight took the torc and held it in both hands as he gazed down at Finn. "Now, in centuries gone, we'd be celebrating this day with song and a feast and many a boastful tale from older apprentices and Knights deep in their cups. But even without the vainglory trappings, 'tis a wondrous moment." He got down on one knee in front of Finn. "'I am the vigor of man,'" he quoted softly, then pulled the torc open just wide enough to slip it around the boy's throat. He squeezed it, bringing the two ends close, but not quite touching. "*Gle mhaith*, lad. Wear it with honest pride. Not many apprentices earn the torc at such a young age."

"Really?" Finn tucked his chin, trying to view the neckpiece.

"Truly. Now go admire yer beauty, then we'll eat."

Tearing out of the kitchen, Finn dashed back to the half-bath. Clicking on the light, he leaned over the sink, his breath fogging the mirror as he adjusted the band. "Gideon!" he yelled over a shoulder. "What about when I shower?" He jumped when the Knight appeared behind him.

"'Tis pure gold. Water can't harm it. Ye might want to remove it to sleep, however."

"No way. I'm never taking it off." Finn grinned up at his master in the mirror.

Gideon smiled back.

The Journal of Finnegan MacCullen: June 19

I did it!!! I bagged my first Amandán!!! Got my torc and everything. Still got it on.

I didn't think I was going to—they're hard to kill. And the fight seemed to go on forever. I hope Gideon didn't notice how scared I was. But then we charged them together and BAM! My knife went in!

Gideon is a freaking machine when he fights!!! He never gets tired. I wonder if I'll ever be as good as he is. Probably not. *Nobody* is as good a warrior as he is.

On the way home, I asked him why he didn't just throw his knife at the goblins. He said the throw is a last-resort move and should never be done unless you have no other options. Because the risk of missing is too great, especially if you don't have an extra blade. I guess that's why we spend so much time practicing stabbing as well as throwing.

What I Learned Today:

The ash or powder Amandán leave behind is like when a snake sheds its skin. That's why it takes time for the creature to reform.

I also learned that humans, like Rafe, feel about their people's heritage like I feel about mine. I guess his lion bracelet is like my torc. I wish I could tell him about it. And what it means.

The Journal of Gideon Lir: June 19

Finnegan MacCullen, after being an apprentice for less than four weeks, won his first battle with an Amandán. It was well-fought. And I doubt I'll see that torc off of him for quite some time.

He does, however, have a ways to go. He is still defiant, still struggles with his temper. But I believe Finn will make a fine Knight in time.

I should have spoken with him this evening about the Steel boy. I know from experience that friendships between mortals and De Danaan only end in sorrow.

But he deserved to have this evening of joy. I'll battle with him tomorrow over breakfast.

Fourteen

"But why?" Finn stood in the middle of the kitchen, breakfast forgotten on the table. He glared at his master's back. "It's not like I'm going to tell him what I am and start waving my knife around. I'm not stupid, you know." His voice rose in frustration.

"What part of *ye're-not-to-associate-with-mortals* are ye not understanding?" Gideon slammed his thick mug into the sink and turned around. Crossing his arms over his chest, he stared down at the boy. "Look, ye want friends. And that's all well and fine. As long as they're *our* kind." He pushed a dirty skillet aside, then leaned back against the counter. "What about Asher?"

"Asher?" Finn made a face. "He's a jerk."

Gideon raised an eyebrow. "'Tis a bit rude."

"I could be ruder," Finn mumbled. "And anyway, Rafe's cool. This summer, he got to visit his grandfather in—"

"No, Finn."

"Oh, come on, Gideon! What's the big deal if I hang out with him once in awhile?"

Gideon's face darkened. Ignoring the question, he snatched a piece of paper off the counter and held it out. "Here's a list of chores and drills ye're to do whilst I pay a visit to Mac Roth and speak with him about—"

"You're not even listening to me!" Finn shoved a kitchen chair against the table with a bang, rattling the leftover dishes. Anger swelled in his chest. He found it hard to breathe.

"I *am* listening to ye. Ye wish to befriend a mortal. And the Steels are decent folk. But the answer is still bleedin' no!" The Knight took a calming breath and threw the sheet of paper on the table as he brushed past Finn. "I want these chores completed by the time I get back at one o'clock," he said over his shoulder as he left.

Finn snatched up the list and crumpled it into a ball. His mouth twisted with frustration as he hurled it across the kitchen. Whirling around, he stormed out the back door.

Stalking across the yard, he headed to the punching bag hanging from a tree limb in the far corner. With a growl, he attacked it with his fists, trying to empty himself of the rage. Pummeling the bag, he focused on his hands striking the leather, relishing the shocks traveling up his arms and into his body. He grunted with each dull *smack*.

After a few minutes, he slowed down, panting, as his mind drifted back to that evening a week ago, when Gideon had first installed the bag. Finn remembered how his master had showed him the correct rhythm of boxing and the proper balance of feet and fists. *Ye might not always have a blade, boyo, so learning a bit of hand-to-hand fighting technique may come in handy.* Taking a deep breath, Finn flexed his hands, shaking them out as he stepped back and watched the bag swing to and fro. As his fury drained away, he heard Gideon's voice inside his head. *And Finn? When yer anger becomes too much, I want ye out here, pummeling this bag. We'll see if we can't channel some of that emotion into something more productive. Like boxing exercises.*

As he stood there, Finn listened to Gideon's truck shuddering to life, the engine protesting as it backed out of their driveway and then drove away. *Guess I should go pick up that stupid list and get busy.* "I wonder who did all the work around here before *I* came?" he grumbled aloud. Licking smarting knuckles, he blew on them as he ambled toward the house. He slipped inside the kitchen and glanced at the table.

The crumpled list rested amongst the dishes, smoothed open. Finn walked over and looked at it. *4. Practice boxing for fifteen minutes* was checked off.

Shoving the pile of dirty clothes under his bed, Finn glanced around his bedroom. *Good enough.* He froze at the faint sound of voices and the clang of the front gate opening and closing. He hurried across the hall and crept over to Gideon's bedroom window.

Peeking out, his eyes widened at the sight of Rafe and Savannah heading along the walk toward the front porch. As he watched, Savannah glanced back over her shoulder at the bronze wire looped over and around the gate. He noticed her hair was pulled back into neat rows of tight braids.

Finn turned and raced down the stairs, reaching the door just as someone knocked. With a guilty twinge in his stomach, he flung it open.

"Hey, Finn," Rafe said. Behind her brother's shoulder, Savannah gave him a smile.

"How's it going?" Finn replied. Trying to act nonchalant, he pushed a discarded knife behind the door with his foot. Its blade was snapped off near the hilt. He stepped aside. "Wanna come in?"

"Actually, we're walking over to the mini-mart to get a slush drink. Do you want to go with us?" Savannah asked.

Finn hesitated for a moment. *Well, I* am *done with everything,* he thought. *And it's only eleven.* "Sure, that'd be great. Let me get some money. You can wait in the living room."

As they walked in, he caught the scent of something flowery or perfume-y when Savannah passed by. "Be right back."

Taking the stairs two at a time, he made a beeline for Gideon's room. He headed over to the dresser. To one side, a handmade terracotta bowl held a moonstone. A layer of dust coated the bowl and stone. Glancing at it, Finn winced as he recalled Gideon's cold tone and hard face when he had asked about it just a few days ago. *'Tis none of yer business, Finnegan MacCullen. It belonged to someone else, and that's all ye need to know.*

Shrugging off the memory, Finn dug a hand into the coin jar on the other end of the dresser. He fished out some quarters and dimes, shoved them in his pocket, then tossed the rest back into the container with a clink. *I know he's saving money for new tires,* he thought, trying to ignore another stab of guilt. *But one soda pop won't hurt.* He went back downstairs to the living room.

"Okay, I'm ready to—" He stopped at Rafe and Savannah's expressions. Brother and sister stood in front of the fireplace, staring up open-mouthed over the mantel, at the rack which held the assortment of weapons.

"These are beyond cool!" Rafe stepped closer. He reached up to touch the hide-wrapped handle of one of the knives. "Are they Mr. Lir's?"

"Uh … yeah. He collects them."

"Are they antiques?" Rafe stood on tiptoe to get a better view of the ones on the top rack.

"I guess. He's had some of them for years. He's got a bunch more stored in the cellar."

"Does he *use* them for anything?" Savannah asked. "Hey, be careful!" She put out a hand to stop her brother from touching the edge of a wicked-looking knife sporting a handle made from deer antler.

"See?" Rafe deliberately dragged a finger along the flat of the blade as he scowled at her. "That's why I didn't want you to tag along. You're such a girl."

"You say it like it's a bad thing. When, in fact, you're envious. Just who kicked whose butt running with Dad this morning?"

Finn shifted his feet nervously. "Hey, guys? Let's go already."

He ushered them out the front. Pausing to lock the door behind him, Finn tucked the house key into his pocket, then followed Rafe and Savannah across the yard and down the street.

Finn's eyes darted from side to side as he examined every shadow. *I feel naked without my knife. But there's no way I could have explained to them why I was packing a blade.* He tried not to think about what Gideon would do if he found out Finn had not only spent time with Rafe and Savannah, but had left home without a weapon.

After making their way to the end of the street, the threesome veered east. They took a shortcut through the mile-long park dividing their neighborhood from the nearby strip mall. A playground area with an enormous picnic pavilion dominated one corner, while several soccer fields stretched across the other side. Dense, rambling groves of trees created islands of shade.

Walking between them, Savannah glanced at Finn's neck. "That's really a neat necklace." She blushed, the rich color of her cheeks deepening. "I mean choker. Or whatever it is that guys wear."

Finn grinned. "It's called a torc. It's a traditional Irish neckpiece. Just for men."

"Is it real gold?" Rafe peered around his sister, trying to get a look at it. He whistled when Finn nodded.

"So are you Irish? Like from Ireland?" Savannah asked.

"No, I was born here in Colorado. But my da was from there. And so is Gideon."

"See, I told you," she bragged to her brother. "Mr. Lir *does* have an accent."

"And it really comes out when he's mad about something," Finn said.

Brother and sister laughed, sharing a knowing smile. "You should hear our mom's."

"Is your da from South Africa, too?"

"St. Louis," Savannah said. "But he likes going every summer, which is their winter. I do, too. This time, my grandfather showed us some fey rings out in the bush that were unreal."

Finn stumbled as he missed a step. "F-fey rings?"

Savannah nodded, the beads in her hair clicking softly. "They're also called fairy rings. They're found in Namibia, Angola, and South Africa. They're these big circles in the dirt where no vegetation grows. Just bare soil. Some are about a yard across, some are a lot bigger. With kind of an ashy dirt. My grandfather has this old friend, Padraic O'Brien, who's been a safari guide for years and *he* says that the local people believe the fey rings are made by some sort of supernatural creatures."

Reaching the deserted pavilion, all three paused in the shade. The boys perched on the top of one of the picnic tables, while Savannah took a seat on the bench, facing them.

"What do *you* think made them?" Finn asked.

"I don't know. But Mr. O'Brien said once…" Her voice trailed off.

"Said what?"

"Well, that they look like…like blast zones. Like something exploded on those spots."

Rafe snorted. "O'Brien's weird. I don't know why Grandfather hangs out with him."

Finn frowned. "Why do you say that?"

"Well, for one thing, he never looks like he's getting any older. And he never goes anywhere, and I mean *anywhere*, without a knife. And he and Grandfather are always exploring those caves in the foothills by his house."

"Well, I think he's cool." Savannah's eyes flashed.

"That's because he tells you all those myths from around the world, and you're such a baby that you still believe in fairies and unicorns and talking animals." Rafe laughed at his sister's mortification. "Oh, yeah. And elves." He turned to Finn. "You should have seen her when the *Lord of the Rings* movies came out." He jerked his knee out of the way as Savannah swung her fist at his leg.

"Shut up, Rafe! I don't *believe* in them. I just think legends like that are…are interesting. Like the stories of Anansi the African trickster. He does all these…"

"Man, stop her before she hurts herself," Rafe muttered under his breath.

Finn faked a laugh, his mind whirling. *I'll bet my torc that Padraic O'Brien is a Tuatha De Danaan. And their grandfather knows it.* He blinked as Rafe slapped him on the back.

"Come on. I hear a purple slush drink calling my name."

With a nod, Finn hopped down and started across the park, the other two lagging behind as Rafe continued teasing his sister. Reaching a broad stand of trees, Finn followed the shadow-dappled path into it as it dipped down into a hollow, the terrain muting traffic noise and the sounds of the distant neighborhood. He turned a corner, then stopped and looked back as he waited for the twins to appear. *Maybe Gideon would let me be friends with them if he knew their grandfather knows about the De Danaan? Talk about the luck of the Irish—I thought stuff like this only happened in books or movies.*

A dark shape dropped past him. It stroked his arm with the tip of its wing before landing on the trail. Finn let out a yelp and jumped sideways. His skin crawled as he stared at the crow. The crow stared back, its head cocked to one side. It gave a harsh caw, then heaved itself back into the air and disappeared into the canopy. A single ebony feather floated down.

"Oh, crap." Finn reached behind himself for his knife. He groaned when his fingers closed on nothing. *Okay, don't panic.* He swiveled around as he tried to scan the woods on either side. Twigs snapped and leaves crunched. A heavy figure suddenly stepped from the trees a few yards in front of him and blocked the path.

"Oh, hello, dear. I'm so sorry if I frightened you. I was just looking for my dog." The pudgy, middle-aged woman, dressed in a jogging outfit, held up a leash and gave it a shake, jingling the clip. "He ran off." She began walking toward him.

Finn backed away, his heart pounding so hard he could feel himself shake. *How am I supposed to know if it's a goblin or not? The Amandán could be anywhere nearby, and this is just some lady. My moonstone doesn't work. I don't have a knife. And even if I did, I can't go around sticking people with it, just to see if they're Amandán or not.* The thoughts careened through his head as he tried to keep a safe distance from the woman.

At that moment, Rafe and Savannah stepped around the far corner, waving their arms and yelling at each other as they approached. Finn glanced over his shoulder, then back at the woman. Is she, or isn't she?

The woman smiled. Her grin stretched wider and wider across her face, as if the corners of her mouth were trying to meet each other around the back of her head. She dropped the leash. With a shudder, she began twisting and contorting. Her jogging outfit melted into a shaggy green pelt. Glancing past Finn's shoulder, the Amandán let out a rough guffaw.

"Good pickings today—fey *and* man flesh." Without warning, it lunged at him, both hands reaching for his face. "*Poc sídhe!*"

Finn leaped backward just in time. He dodged around the Amandán as it lunged for him again. *I got to keep it away from Rafe and Savannah!* He dove for a fallen branch lying on the ground. Rolling to his feet, he came up swinging and aimed a blow at the goblin's head. The branch whistled through empty air as the Amandán ducked.

Out of the corner of his eye, he spied the Steels standing almost nose to nose, still arguing, unaware of the goblin. The Amandán laughed. With one last glance at his friends, Finn threw the branch at his foe. "Come and get me, ugly," he shouted, then turned and plunged into the woods.

Fifteen

Branches lashed at Finn as he tore through the underbrush, one arm bent before his face, shielding his eyes. The torc bounced against his collar bone. Dead vegetation crunched underfoot, almost drowning out the Amandán's raspy breathing as it chased after him. Not daring to look back, he angled further away from the path. Once, he stumbled when he snagged his toes on an exposed root. Wind-milling his arms, he managed to stay on his feet. He cried out as the creature's fingers snagged the back of his tee shirt. With a desperate lunge, he jerked free.

Wheezing for air, he burst out of the copse of trees and raced across the adjoining soccer field. The thud of pursuing feet echoed the pounding of his heart. His legs and lungs burning, he began chanting. "'I am a wind on the sea'." Each syllable was a puff of air.

For a moment, nothing happened.

Then, swiftness poured into his legs like a river in springtime flood. Lengthening his stride, he sped up, the goblin's footsteps fading behind him. As he flew along, the wind blew his hair off his forehead. He laughed from relief and risked a peek backwards.

And tripped over a sprinkler head.

Finn slammed, shoulder first, into the ground, one arm twisted beneath him. Searing pain shot along his wrist. Breathless from the hurt, he rolled over. He scrabbled backward on his elbows and heels, certain the goblin was right on top of him. Panting, he looked around.

The park was empty.

"Finn!"

His pulse thundering in his ears, Finn shook his hair out of his eyes. The twins ran toward him, Savannah in the lead, braids flying. Holding his wrist, he staggered to his feet just as they skidded to a halt in front of him.

"What the heck was that all about?" Rafe said. "We thought we saw someone chasing you through the trees."

Savannah looked around. "Yeah, and where'd they go?"

Cradling his left arm, Finn shrugged, then grimaced, the injured limb protesting the movement. "Aw, it was just some lady. She said she lost her dog and then she freaked out and started running after me."

"Well, maybe she thought you had it, or something." Rafe shook his head. "But talk about overreacting."

Savannah narrowed her eyes as she studied Finn's face and the way he held his arm. "You look kinda pale. Well, more pale than usual. Maybe Mom should check your wrist. You might have sprained it, or even broken it."

Ignoring the throbbing pain, Finn let go of his arm. "Naw, I'm good. It's feeling better already." He leaned over and brushed the grass off his jeans with his good hand, trying to act nonchalant. *Last thing I need is Dr. Steel fussing over me. She'd probably tell Gideon and then all you-know-what would break loose.* He checked his watch. "Look, I better get back. I need to finish some stuff. Um ... thanks anyway. I'll see you around."

Without waiting for an answer, Finn turned and headed home. *Maybe this is why Gideon didn't want me to have humans as friends,* he thought as he walked along, his wrist aching more and more with every step.

I just put them in danger. Made them targets for the goblin, too. Still, it would've been nice to get to hang out with Rafe once in a while.

After a few yards, he tensed at the swish of running feet behind him. Before he could turn around, Rafe and Savannah had caught up with him. They slowed and flanked him on either side.

"Not so fast." Rafe thumped Finn on the shoulder, ignoring his gasp of pain. He strolled along, matching Finn's stride "Do you really think we're going to let you walk home alone after some crazy lady chases you clear across the park?"

"And with a possible broken wrist," Savannah added. "Sorry, Finn, but we're not buying your tough guy routine." She smiled up at him.

He ducked his head and grinned.

"Later!" After a final wave, Finn hurried up the walk to his house. Unlocking the door one-handed, he slipped inside and nudged it closed with his heel. He wiped the sweat off his forehead in relief. *Ye gods, talk about relentless. Good thing I finally convinced Savannah that I was okay.*

I don't think it's broken, but it sure hurts like heck. He tried moving it, hissing at the stabbing pain shooting up his arm. *What am I going to tell Gideon?*

He walked into the living room. Toeing off his shoes, he kicked them aside and flopped onto the worn sofa. With a groan, he slouched further down and stared at the stone fireplace.

Three times, he thought. *That's three times I've been ambushed by an Amandán. Is that normal? If I ask Gideon about it, then he'll know I took off with Rafe and Savannah.*

Lifting his eyes, he gazed at the weapons above the mantel. *I've got to come up with some way of telling Amandán from mortals.* Digging into a pocket with his good hand, he slipped out his father's stone and held it up between thumb and forefinger as he gazed at its creamy surface.

"Ye know, it would be bleedin' helpful if ye worked for me."
Making a face, he tucked it away. *Great,* he thought, glancing at the
Knight's desk tucked in the corner. *Now, I'm starting to* sound *like him.*

With a weary sigh, he toppled over onto his right side. Curling up,
he shoved a pillow against his stomach and rested the injured arm
on it, then closed his eyes. *I'm glad I was able to lead it away from Rafe
and Savannah. I've got be careful around them. Especially with the increasing
attacks. No matter what, I'm carrying my knife next time I'm with them.* He
yawned, then smiled to himself as his eyes shut. *And there'll be a next
time.*

Gideon stood in the middle of the living room, a puzzled
expression on his face as he watched Finn sleep. *I did not think the chore
list was* that *tiresome,* he thought. He stepped closer and frowned as he
noticed the boy's left arm. *And just how hard were you punching that bag?*
Taking a seat on the nearby coffee table, he patted his apprentice's
knee. "Wake up, boyo."

Finn blinked and looked around blearily. "What's wrong?" he
said, in confusion. He sat up gingerly, trying to tame his rumpled
hair with his good hand.

"I should ask ye." Leaning over, Gideon slid a hand under Finn's
swollen wrist, supporting the boy's arm as he peered at it. "Boxing a
bit too enthusiastically?"

"Uh...yeah. I guess I went after it pretty hard."

Gideon flexed Finn's wrist a few times, and raised an eyebrow
at Finn's yelp. "It's just a sprain, ye wee baby," he teased. "And ye
call yerself a De Danaan—maybe I should take that torc back." He
released Finn's arm and rose. "We'll apply a cooling poultice, and
then I'll wrap it for ye. T'will be right as rain by tomorrow." He
headed for the kitchen, the apprentice on his heels.

While Finn took a seat at the kitchen table, Gideon soaked a rag
in a wide-mouthed jar of *slainte* nettle brew he kept in the refrigerator.

"Keep the cloth draped around yer wrist until 'tis no longer cold," Gideon instructed him as he bustled around preparing sandwiches. Carrying lunch to the table, he handed one of the plates to Finn and joined him. "By the way, I've a bit of news for ye." He took a bite of his roast beef sandwich, and grunted with approval as he licked mustard off his thumb.

"We're getting a computer?" Finn's face lit up. "Finally! Even sharing with my cousins was better than—" He stopped when Gideon shook his head.

"Ye know how tight our budget is. The value of gold is low right now, so our monthly stipend is low. Once the global market for gold picks up, we'll look into getting one, eh?"

Finn nodded. He scooped up a handful of potato chips and shoved them into his mouth. "So, how does that work?" he asked, crumbs sputtering out of his mouth. "I mean, do we really get a pile of gold each month?"

"Finnegan MacCullen! For the hundredth time, do not speak whilst eating! Ye gods, it's like living with a feral child. I should just tie ye up to a post in the backyard and feed ye out of a bowl on the ground." He shook his head when Finn burst out laughing, choking on his food and spewing even more crumbs.

"Now, to answer yer question, all De Danaan receive a set amount of funds deposited into their bank accounts each month from a common reserve. That reserve is based on gold accumulated from trade as well as plunder in the ancient days. Mac Roth believes that's where the Irish legend of the leprechaun's pot of gold at the end of the rainbow might have come from."

"But we're Tuatha De Danaan. Fey, not leprechauns."

"Aye, but mortals have twisted and blended truth and legend so much that very few, if any, humans know or understand that other beings share this world."

Finn began to speak, then stopped and stuffed the last of the sandwich in his mouth. Careful to swallow before talking, he asked. "So, what was the news?"

"Mac Roth and Asher will be hunting more often with us."

He made a face. "Why?"

Gideon gazed across the table for a moment, his eyes glancing at the torc around Finn's neck, and then down to his injured arm. "For protection."

"Protection?"

"Aye. With the beasties becoming bolder, there is safety in numbers." He rose. Gathering the empty plates, he placed them in the sink and began running the water. Speaking over his shoulder, he added, "So, we've decided to band together. That way, Mac Roth and I can hunt more productively and provide additional supervision for ye two hooligans." He flipped a towel over one arm and started to wash, then raised his eyebrows when Finn joined him, elbowing him aside.

"I got it. I made that promise, remember?" Finn explained. He paused at Gideon's look of astonishment. "What?"

"Why, nothing. Nothing at all." The Knight smiled to himself and draped the towel over Finn's shoulder. "Keep yer injured wrist out of the warm water if ye can."

"Yes, sir." Finn grinned when Gideon cuffed him affectionately, his hand lingering on the boy's head for a moment.

"Good lad."

"Right. Grip it tight, now," Gideon instructed. He began pounding in another nail, anchoring a narrow strip of bronze sheeting to the window sill. The *twonk-twonk* of each hammer strike rebounded off the glass pane and echoed around their front porch.

Standing shoulder to shoulder with his master, Finn held the metal in place with his good hand. As Gideon worked, Finn watched him out of the corner of his eye.

Stripped down to a white tee shirt, the Knight swung the hammer with short, controlled strikes, his brows drawn together in concentration. Finn studied the muscles in Gideon's arms, then glanced down at his own and made a face. *I wonder if I should start lifting weights or something. I look like a drawing of a stick figure.*

"So, how long did it take to get that?" he asked, gesturing with his chin at Gideon's tattoo.

"Twelve years and one hour," Gideon said, around the extra nail held between his teeth.

"T-twelve years?"

"The length of my apprenticeship, plus the hour it took the druid to mark me."

"Can *I* get one when I finish my apprenticeship?" *I'll have a tattoo like my da,* he thought. *And Gideon, too,* a quiet voice added.

Gideon spat the nail into his palm before answering. "Aye. If ye can abide the prick of the thorn."

Finn's eyes bulged. "A *thorn?*" To his embarrassment, his voice cracked.

Gideon nodded, his attention on the task. "If yer going to carry the mark of Knighthood, ye should be tattooed in the old way." He swung the hammer again. "There. That was the last one." Thunder rumbled overhead as an afternoon storm built up over the western mountains.

"Will this really stop the Amandán from getting inside the house?" Finn stepped back to the edge of the porch, studying the pair of windows next to the front entrance. "Because it looks totally stupid. Especially the door."

Gideon wiped the sweat from his face with the hem of his tee shirt. "Nonsense. This is going to be the next home decorating trend," he said, tossing the hammer into the toolbox with a clang. "Why, soon everyone will be framing their windows in bronze as well as sheathing their doors with it." He glanced down the path. "By the way, well done on the gate. Clever solution to—" He stopped, staring at the three figures approaching from across the street. "Now, what would they be wanting?" he muttered, walking down the steps.

Finn spun around at the Knight's comment. *Oh, no—not now, Rafe.* He plucked nervously at the elastic bandage wrapped around his left wrist.

"Hey, Finn!" Rafe called, as they drew nearer. "My dad wanted to meet you and ask you about that woman that chased you."

"And to make sure your arm was okay," Savannah added.

The twins' father stepped forward. "Hello, Gideon. Good to see you again." He shook hands with the reluctant De Danaan, trying not to stare at the bronze-covered door behind Finn. "And you must be Finn MacCullen, right?"

"Yes, sir," Finn said through stiff lips, frozen in place on the porch.

The Knight cleared his throat. "How might I be of service, Rufus?"

Rufus Steel smiled, draping an arm around Savannah's shoulders. "Oh, I just wanted to stop by and check on Finn. And I was wondering if he could tell me more about what happened at the park this morning?"

"Beg pardon—the park? This morning?"

"Yes, when he and my children went to the store for sodas."

Gideon stiffened. Without turning his head, he spoke over his shoulder. "Come." The Knight pointed the ground next to his right side. "Here."

I am so screwed, Finn thought, as he started down the steps.

Sixteen

The Journal of Finnegan MacCullen: June 20

Day one hundred and sixty-two of my captivity...

Gideon would call that *hyperbole*.

I'm serving prison time. In my room. I *think* I'm grounded until the autumn equinox, but it was hard to understand him. When Gideon's really angry, his accent goes off the scale! At least he didn't blow up in front of Rafe and Savannah—he waited until they left.

Mr. Steel's a science teacher, not a policeman or anything. So, I don't understand why he kept asking me if I felt safe in the neighborhood, and if anyone had ever chased me before.

Gee, Mr. Steel. Do ugly, smelly goblins that want to scramble my brains inside of my skull count as *unsafe*?

<u>What I Learned Today:</u>

Omission of the truth is a falsehood, according to Gideon. By sneaking off with Rafe and Savannah after he told me no, and by letting him believe that I hurt myself boxing instead of escaping an Amandán, it was like lying to him.

Don't think I'll be making *that* mistake again!

It's weird.

I really, really want to be friends with Rafe and Savannah. (Mostly Rafe. Savannah's okay for a girl.) And I thought I was cool with disobeying Gideon about it. I mean, being buds with Rafe can't hurt anyone.

Not if I'm careful.

But I really, really want Gideon to trust me. To think I'm a good apprentice.

To like me. And not just because I'm his apprentice.

But to like *me*.

It's late. Almost midnight. Still raining, but not as hard.

Gideon's not back yet.

He went hunting by himself in the park where that goblin chased me today. Headed over there right after dark to try to pick up its trail and track it.

What if there's more than one Amandán? What if he's hurt right now, out in this storm, and I'm just sitting around?

That's it—I'm out of here!!!

Finn closed the journal with a *clap*. Jumping up, he fished his shoes out from under the desk and shoved his feet into them, hopping on one foot, then the other, as he tied them. He flexed his wrist a few times. *Not too bad, I guess.* He hurried from the room and down the stairs to the living room. Halting in front of the weapon rack, he selected a knife. "Hmm, I better take an extra," he muttered, grabbing a second one. He thrust one into his belt at his hip and the other in the sheath, then took a deep breath and headed toward the front door. Grabbing his hoodie from the coat hook, he tugged it on and slipped outside.

Breaking into a jog, he pulled the hood up against the rain and glanced around the neighborhood. He splashed along, hunching his shoulders each time the lightning cracked. Finn couldn't help noticing the lit windows of the other houses on the street. *All those humans. Safe inside their homes. And none of them know about our war with the Amandán. I wonder if any one of them would even help us.*

Reaching the edge of the park, he slowed down and pushed the hood back. Panting, he listened intently as he tried to slow his breathing. A faint shout jerked his head around. He squinted as he peered through the storm at the far side of the park.

A beam of light danced about, illuminating the inside of the open-air pavilion. On top of one of the picnic tables, a familiar figure held a moonstone high in one hand as he swung a blade at the shapes rampaging below.

"Gideon," Finn whispered. He watched in horror as one of the Amandán leaped up on the table behind the Knight. Before he could shout a warning, his master twisted around and buried his blade in its chest. The goblin disappeared in a silent explosion of gray powder.

Finn sprinted across the park. *Two left,* he thought as he ran, water spraying out from under his feet. *We can handle two. I just got to get up there with him.* The fear of arriving too late nipped at his heels.

When he reached the edge of the pavilion, the light vanished. Finn blinked as his eyes adjusted to the darkness. Chest heaving, he pressed himself against one of the thick concrete posts holding up the roof and wiped the rain from his face, then slipped a knife out of his belt. *I've got to time this just right. Make a run for the table when those monsters aren't looking.* He waited, bouncing on his toes as he studied the distance between himself and the picnic bench.

The Knight smiled grimly while the two goblins circled around below him. "A wee leery of attacking me straight on, eh?" He wiped the sweat and ash from his eyes with the back of a hand. "Since I took out two of yer cronies?" He tightened his grip on the knives. The rain hammered on the metal roof, muffling the creatures' growls and insults.

From the corner of his eye, he caught a dark shape darting out from behind a nearby pillar. He cursed as something landed behind him with a thud, the table rocking underfoot. He staggered, then spun around and slashed at the new threat. With a cry, the figure dropped to its knees.

"Gideon—it's me!" Finn crouched low, a knife in one hand. He peeked up at the Knight. "Um…hi."

"Finn! What the bleedin 'ell are ye doing here?" he roared, then lunged over the apprentice's head to stab at the goblin that had started creeping up on the bench behind the boy. The creature jerked back to avoid the blade and stumbled, falling to the concrete pad with a yelp.

To Gideon's astonishment, Finn crawled between his legs and scrambled to the far end of the table. Raising his knife, he plunged it into the other Amandán's hand as it reached for the Knight's ankle, and pinned it to the wooden surface. The creature shrieked. It wrenched its limb to and fro, trying to free itself.

"I'm helping you," Finn shouted back. He scooted over until his shoulder pressed against Gideon's knee, cradling his injured wrist.

"Ye gods, stand up! I'm going to trip over ye, and ye're no bleedin' good down there!"

As Finn lurched to his feet, Gideon suddenly grabbed the top of the boy's head and shoved him back down again. With a flick of his wrist, the Knight sent a knife into the chest of the goblin attempting to free its companion. A moment later, he slammed the second blade into the pinned creature. Both Amandán exploded, sending a double portion of ash everywhere.

Reaching over, Finn pried his weapon loose from the table with a grunt. He stood up, pulled the second knife from his belt, and passed it to the Knight. Both armed, they braced for another attack.

Quiet fell over the area, broken only by the pinging of rain on the metal roof.

After a few minutes, Gideon dug the moonstone back out of his pocket and raised it high, scanning the bushes and trees around them. A final rumble sounded from the sky as the storm began to diminish.

"All clear." Tucking the stone away, Gideon turned around, his face hard. "What, in the name of the Goddess Danu, am I to do with ye?"

Finn shook his dripping hair out of his eyes and squared his shoulders. "Look, I know you're mad at me. *Again.* But I don't care. Because there's no way I am going to let you hunt by yourself." He locked eyes with Gideon and waited.

The Knight sighed and rubbed his knuckles along his jaw as he studied the young face. *Ye gods, the lad reminds me so much of myself at this age. Stubborn, temperamental, and already befriending a mortal. How can I punish him for acting the same way I did?* He smiled to himself. *If only my old master could see this now.*

"Perhaps ye were right to follow me, boyo." Gideon chuckled when Finn's mouth sagged open. "I probably shouldn't have hunted alone." He reached out to tap the boy's torc with the handle of his knife. "Not when there's another warrior in our home." He stepped off the table and onto the bench, then to the ground. Finn followed with a hop and a grin.

"So, does this mean I'm not grounded anymore?" He hurried to collect the Knight's blades, careful to wipe them clean on his soaked jeans.

"I suppose not. Maybe I should just beat ye black and blue instead. With a bleedin' hard stick." He took the weapons, keeping one in each hand.

"Yeah, right," Finn scoffed.

They left the pavilion to go home. The drizzle washed their faces and clothes, leaving streaks of damp ash. Finn lengthened his stride as he tried to match the Knight's. For a few minutes, they squelched along in silence.

"Um…Gideon?"

"Yes?"

"I'm sorry I lied. About Rafe and my wrist and all that." He held up his arm, the elastic bandage filthy with goblin remains and mud.

Gideon nodded. "Apology accepted. And we best rewrap that wrist again when we get home. We'll talk in the morning about the Steel children. Perhaps we can come to some agreement, ye and me." He glanced down at Finn. "Ye understand, do ye now, that being friends with you might be dangerous to *them?* The Amandán are quite happy to hunt down any mortal they perceive as our ally."

"Yes, sir, I get it. And I like Rafe. And Savannah. But I don't want them to get hurt." He looked around in the darkness, then overhead, watching the stars when they appeared between shreds of clouds. "Things are going to get worse, aren't they? For us De Danaan?"

The Knight hooked an arm around the boy's shoulders. "Aye, lad. Much worse. So, promise me something." He stopped and pulled Finn to a halt, one hand still on his shoulder.

"What?"

"Ye're never to put yerself in danger to protect me, such as ye did this evening. Now, do I have yer word?"

Finn glanced away. He hesitated for a moment, then shook his head. "I can't make that promise, Gideon. I'm sorry."

Nor would I have, at his age. The Knight shrugged. "I dinna think ye would, but I had to try." He turned again for home, the boy by his side.

"How did you know I wouldn't?"

"Because for good or for bad, me old master's fondest desire has come true."

"Which is, what?"

"That the Fates send me an apprentice exactly like meself."

The Journal of Gideon Lir: June 20

The Celts have always believed that life is a Circle. An unending, repeating pattern that twists and turns and brings us back to the beginning.

And if that is so, then it must stand to reason that Finnegan MacCullen was destined to be my apprentice. And I his master.

But now we are also friends. A great gift, to be sure.

Perhaps the greatest gift in this round world.

Seventeen

Fidgeting beside Gideon as his master spoke with the bank teller, Finn eyed the pen attached to a chain on the counter. Picking it up, he swung it back and forth a few times. After a few swings, he began twirling it around, faster and faster. *I wonder if I could get it to hum.* He spun it harder, picking up speed. The chain made a rhythmic clinking.

He yelped when a work boot kicked him in the ankle. "Ow." Glaring over at his master, he let the chain wrap itself around his hand before putting the pen back down. "That hurt."

"Aye, I'm sure it did." Gideon gave a polite nod to the teller as she handed him a deposit slip and some money. Stepping away from the counter, he checked the paper, then folded it in half and tucked it in his pocket. He kept a couple of bills in one hand. "Thank the gods 'tis the first of the month. June was just a bit too tight, financially."

"No kidding." Finn followed his master across the lobby and through the heavy glass doors. Colorado's combination of high, thin air and summer sun was already cooking High Springs' downtown.

"But, I've good news, boyo."

"Computer?"

"Still no." Before Finn could question him further, a cultured voice spoke behind them.

"Why, good morning, Gideon Lir."

They turned around. A tall, white-haired man, accompanied by an older teenage boy, was walking toward them. The boy's eyes, a rich brown that matched his hair, were filled with curiosity as he gazed at Finn.

"And to ye, Basil," Gideon said in way of a greeting. As he chatted with the other man, the boy sauntered over to Finn.

"How's it going?"

"Okay," Finn replied.

"I'm Griffin, Basil's apprentice," he said. Tilting his head to one side, he studied Finn. "You're a Tuatha De Danaan, aren't you?"

"H-how did you know?" *He even pronounced it right,* thought Finn.

"Oh, Basil told me about your people once. You two hunt monsters, or something?"

"Uh, yeah. A kind of goblin," Finn said vaguely. "Did...did you say you were an *apprentice*?"

"Yup. Basil's my Mentor. What you might call a master."

For a long minute, Finn stared at Griffin, who waited with a trace of amusement. He licked his lips in confusion. "Are you guys...you know..."

"Human?" The other teen supplied for him. He shook his head. "Actually, we're angels."

Finn blinked. "Angels."

"That's right." Griffin grinned, his brown eyes crinkling at the corners. "The very top of the supernatural hierarchy, you might say. Basil and I are Terrae Angeli—guardian angels who control the four elements. My specialties are Earth and Fire." He held up a hand and snapped his fingers. With a whoosh, flames ignited and began dancing along their tips. "Especially Fire."

"Whoa!" Finn took a step back. "How did you—"

At that moment, Basil summoned Griffin. Clenching his hand into a fist, he extinguished the flames and hurried away.

Finn joined his master. They watched as the other two walked into the bank. Pausing in the doorway to let Basil enter first, Griffin looked back over his shoulder. He gave a nod and disappeared inside.

"Are they really...?" Finn flapped his arms up and down.

"Aye, that they are," Gideon said. "I usually find Terrae Angeli a bit pretentious, but Basil is a right decent bloke. Down to earth, ye might say."

"I didn't think angels really existed. And lived here, in High Springs."

"Oh, ye'd be surprised who else shares the city with us," Gideon said. He strode along the sidewalk toward their truck, Finn on his heels.

"So, what's the good news you were going to tell me?"

"We have adequate funds to purchase food, clothing, gas, and pay all our bills. And even a wee bit left over. Ye may have these." Gideon handed him two ten-dollar bills.

"What's this for?"

"*Thank ye, Gideon*," said Gideon. He glanced over, one eyebrow raised, and waited.

Finn stared back. "What?" He shoved the money into his pocket, then ducked as Gideon aimed a swipe at his head. "Oh. Yeah. Uh, thanks."

The Knight sighed. "I believe, oh, clueless apprentice, that it is customary for human teenagers to have some spending money."

"What do you mean, *human* teenagers?"

"Ye'll need to act the part if ye're going to have a mortal as a friend." Reaching their vehicle, he unlocked the door and climbed inside. Finn joined him in the cab.

"Hey, thanks again for letting me hang out with Rafe," Finn said with a grin. "He asked me to come over later."

Gideon coaxed the engine on and checked the side mirror as he edged into traffic. "Be careful not to wear out yer welcome." He raised his voice over the truck's grumble. "In fact, toward that end, I want ye home today."

"Why?"

"Because Mac Roth is meeting with Iona today about some new information she's uncovered. Something that might help us finally locate the Spear." His jaw muscle twitched. "We certainly need it now, more than ever."

"Why aren't you meeting with her, too?"

The Knight shifted in his seat. "I have nothing to say to her." As Finn started to press, Gideon growled, "Leave it be, boyo. I mean it." Changing the subject, he added, "So, Asher's going to be with us for a few hours. It would be good for ye to train with another apprentice."

Finn made a face. "It's bad enough we have to hunt with him. Now we have to babysit the creep?"

Gideon frowned as he glanced over at Finn's sullen face. "And just why do ye two dislike each other so much?"

"Because, he's a jerk."

"And ye, an innocent lamb?"

"Pretty much."

"So, ye do nothing to bait him? Like call him *Ass-her*?"

Finn blushed and said nothing.

"That's what I thought," Gideon said as he drove home.

Eighteen

"Get the door," Gideon said, at the loud thump echoing through the house. He stood rummaging through a stack of papers on his desk. "And stop complaining. 'Twill not kill ye to spend an afternoon with Asher."

"It might," replied Finn, from the depths of the sofa. "Then, you'd feel really bad." He clicked off the television set and hauled himself to his feet. Stumping over, he opened the door. "*Fáilte*," he greeted the giant waiting on the porch.

"And to ye, young Finn," boomed Mac Roth, his flaming beard wreathing his wide smile as he stepped inside. He reached out a massive paw. Grabbing the boy's chin, he tipped Finn's head back. "'Tis a fine torc ye're wearing. Did ye steal it, now?"

Finn grinned, eyes dancing as Mac Roth let go. "Aye, I did," he replied, heavy on the accent. "Is yers missing?"

Mac Roth roared with laughter. "Oh, the wee one has a glib tongue." Still chuckling, he glanced over his shoulder as Asher joined them.

The boys locked eyes. A chilly silence filled the space between them. The Knights exchanged glances across the room and shook their heads.

"Well, I best be off." Mac Roth turned to his apprentice. "Behave. Or Knight Lir will kick yer arse. And then I will."

"But Mac..." Asher pleaded, but stopped when his master raised a hand.

"We're not having this conversation again, boyo." Mac Roth lowered his head. He spoke softly to Asher, one hand dwarfing the apprentice's shoulder. "I'd rather ye not be home alone if at all possible, lad." He grinned when Asher grumbled under his breath.

"Here is the list ye asked me about," Gideon said, passing it over to the other Knight. "I'm afraid it is not very accurate, nor up to date."

Glancing down at the sheet, Mac Roth nodded, then folded it in half and tucked it inside his leather jacket. "'Tis a start, for now." With a wave, he turned and left. The Jeep rumbled away a few moments later.

Finn crowded past Asher as he went to close the door. "You wanna get out of the way?" he muttered out of the corner of his mouth.

"You wanna shut up?" Asher hissed back. He elbowed Finn in the ribs as he walked past.

With a growl, Finn shoved him backwards. Before Asher could retaliate, Gideon stepped closer and grabbed them both by the backs of their necks. He gave each a shake.

"Enough," he said, in a stern voice. "Now, outside with ye." Releasing them with another shake, he led the way across the house, through the kitchen, and out the back door. A flawless summer day awaited them.

Gideon nodded toward the far wall. "Finn, twenty leaps, and I want them cleanly done. Over and back counts as two, but no touching the top stones."

As Finn jogged over to the fence to begin his routine, Gideon pointed at a wooden target nailed to the side of the house, its red and blue painted circles chipped and scarred. "Asher, knife throwing practice until Finn is done. Then, ye two switch activities." He waited until Asher slipped two blades free and stepped twenty paces from the target. "I'll be back shortly." He spun on his heels and went back inside.

Ignoring the *thunk* of the other apprentice's knife as it struck the target, Finn focused on the exercise, trying to make each leap without touching. By the last jump, his legs were concrete. His lungs burned as he gasped the line from the Song. Pushing off the ground on the far side of the wall, he knew in mid-air he wasn't going to make it. His toes snagged the top of the wall as he sailed over. With an *oof*, he landed on his hands and knees, and collapsed. For a moment, he lay sprawled on the lawn, wheezing.

"Oh, real smooth, halfer." Asher stood in the far corner, watching. "Is that how you earned your torc? By *falling* on the goblin?"

Finn rolled to his feet and wiped the sweat off his face. "At least I *have* a torc," he panted, resting his hands on top of his head as he walked around, catching his breath. "And I, unlike someone else, don't need a babysitter."

Asher narrowed his eyes, juggling the knives. He grasped the tip of one of them between fingers and thumb. Cocking his arm back, he threw it, end over end, toward the target. The knife impaled the dead center of the bull's eye. "I bet you can't do that." Before Finn could reply, the side gate banged open. A voice called out.

"Hey, Finn! You back here?" Rafe strolled around the corner of the house. "I wanted to see if..." His voice trailed off when he saw the various training apparatuses scattered around the yard, and the knife in Asher's hand. "Whoa. What's all this for?"

"Hi, Rafe." Finn gestured at the items. "Oh, we're just...messing around." He walked over to his friend and aimed a punch at his stomach.

Rafe laughed and blocked it with a flip of his arm. "Who's that?" he asked, nodding toward Asher. He watched with interest as the other boy threw again. "Wow, he's good."

"Um...that's...my cousin. Asher." Finn leaned closer to Rafe. "He's a jerk. I call him 'Ass-her'," he whispered. They grinned at each other.

"Well, well," Asher drawled as he sauntered over. He stopped a few feet away, and studied Rafe up and down for a moment. "Gideon lets you hang out with his kind?"

The amusement died in Rafe's face. He started to say something, then whirled around and stalked away.

"You're dead meat," Finn snarled at Asher. He turned and ran after his friend. "Rafe—wait a sec!" He caught up with the other boy by the side of the house and grabbed his arm, pulling him to a stop. "Look, he's a butt, okay? Just ignore him."

"No big deal." Rafe jerked his arm free. "The world's full of racists," he said, not looking at Finn. Hurt flickered in his black eyes. Without another word, he walked away.

Finn watched his friend's taut back. The look on Rafe's face tore at him. Righteous anger swelled his chest and pushed up into his throat. He spun around and stiff-legged it toward the backyard. A dark haze began flooding the edge of his vision. For a brief second, he tried to control his fury, to take a breath, to count to ten, even count to one hundred. To think about something else. All the strategies Gideon had taught him.

Too late.

The warp spasm sank its claws into him, and took over.

Rounding the corner of the house, he broke into a sprint. As Asher looked up from examining the target, a sneer still on his face, Finn picked up speed. A roar burst from his mouth.

"I am a boar enraged!"

Nineteen

"Ye gods!" Gideon dashed across the yard toward the two boys thrashing on the ground, locked in combat. He threw his arms around Finn and lifted him off his feet. Finn struggled, kicking his legs and flailing his arms. Wincing from an elbow to the ribs, Gideon shouted at Asher. "O'Neill, go in the house! Now!"

Asher rolled over to his side, blood oozing from his nose and mouth, one eye already swelling shut. He lurched to his feet, swaying, then staggered toward the door.

"Let me go," Finn screamed. Dirt and blood from a split lip streaked his chin. With an abrupt twist, he ripped free of the Knight's hold and bolted after his foe.

"Oh, no, ye don't!" Gideon snagged the back of Finn's tee shirt. He dug in his heels, slowing his apprentice long enough for Asher to escape indoors. The back door slammed shut.

Spitting with rage, Finn spun around, wild-eyed with the warp spasm. He swung a fist at Gideon. The Knight blocked the blow with practiced ease. Grabbing Finn's wrist, he hooked his foot around the back of the boy's ankle. With a quick twist, he tumbled him to the ground.

"Now, ye just stay down there, boyo," Gideon said. He dropped to one knee beside his apprentice, and pinned him to the ground with a hand to the chest.

"I'm gonna kill him!" Finn growled as he fought to rise.

"No, ye're not. Ye're going to take a deep breath and tell me what happened."

Finn glared up at his master, blinking back tears of anger. He squeezed his eyes tight as he struggled to calm himself. "He...he told Rafe..." He coughed and turned his head, spitting blood.

"Here. Sit up before ye choke." Gideon grabbed Finn's elbow and pulled him up.

Finn slumped over and rested his forehead on upraised knees, trembling as the warp spasm slowly drained away. In a muffled voice, he explained what had happened. Lifting his face, still white with fury, he looked at the Knight kneeling beside him. "I hate him. I wish he was dead."

"No, ye don't. Violence is never the solution to any problem." He snorted and looked away. "And yet, ironically, I spend me days teaching ye how to hunt and destroy other creatures."

"Yeah, but Amandán aren't like us." Finn pulled up the neck of his tee, wincing as he dabbed at a cut lip. "They're more like animals."

"The same thing was once said of Rafe's ancestors," Gideon reminded him. "Perhaps we are making the same mistake with the Amandán?"

Before Finn could answer, a low mechanical growl saturated the quiet of the neighborhood. They exchanged glances at the sound of Mac Roth's Jeep pulling into the driveway, its tires crunching on the gravel.

"Now, why would Mac Roth be back so early?" Gideon muttered. He rose and dusted the grass off his jeans, then looked down at Finn, still huddled on the lawn. "Stay put until ye have that temper under control."

Finn blew out a breath. "I'm good." He examined his battered knuckles. "I guess all that boxing practice came in handy after all."

Reaching down, Gideon snagged the boy's arm and hauled him to his feet. "I understand ye were defending Rafe. Yer motive was honorable, but yer method was less so." They crossed the yard and reached the back door just as Mac Roth flung it open.

"I'm gone for less than an hour, and I miss a party!"

"I should have kept a closer eye on these two." Gideon ushered Finn in ahead of him.

"Ah, 'tis healthy for young pups to battle it out. Remember all the brawls we had as lads?" Mac Roth stepped to one side as the Knight and his apprentice entered. "Asher has already admitted his part in this."

Asher sat at the table, holding a dripping cloth to one side of his face. The earthy aroma of *slainte* nettle filled the kitchen. He glowered at Finn with his good eye, his face streaked with grime and blood.

"Sit." Gideon pushed Finn toward the opposite chair. He dug in a drawer for another rag, then dipped it in the jar already opened on the counter. After wringing it out, he handed it to Finn.

Finn sighed in relief as the cold poultice soothed his throbbing lip. He held it in place as Mac Roth joined them at the table.

"'Tis a good practice to keep a jar of the brew in the refrigerator, Lir. Especially with these hooligans around. Speaking of which," Mac Roth fixed his gaze on his apprentice. "So, Asher O'Neill. Ye finally ran up against someone who dinna appreciate yer sharp tongue. Apologize for insulting his friend."

"Sorry," Asher said curtly. "And just so you know, I meant *his kind* as in him being a human, not because he's black."

"Whatever," Finn replied. He rolled his eyes when Gideon cleared his throat behind him. "I mean, I accept your apology. And I'm sorry, too." *Yeah*, he thought to himself, *I'm sorry I didn't hit you harder.*

"I suppose that's the best we can hope for," Gideon said. He screwed the lid back on the *slainte* nettle brew and returned it to the refrigerator.

Taking a seat with the others, he raised an eyebrow at Mac Roth. "So, was Iona able to provide us with more information?"

"She mostly confirmed what we already know." Mac Roth pulled Gideon's paper from his pocket, the boys' fight dismissed. "That, supposedly, the Spear was forged centuries ago by the Black Hand and his mortal ally to be the most deadly weapon against the Amandán."

"Does Iona really think it's here? In High Springs?" Finn asked.

"Aye, she does. And she seems certain that it is in Gideon's possession." Mac Roth's eyes gleamed with a wicked light. "She asked after ye, by the way."

"I don't believe I care," Gideon replied, with an icy tone.

Asher peered around his rag. "Why does Iona think *he* has it?"

Mac Roth nodded toward the other Knight, who shifted in his chair. "Not only does Knight Lir have an extensive collection of antique blades, most of which are probably still stored in yer cellar, eh?"

Gideon shrugged. "I detest unpacking."

"But," Mac Roth continued, "he is also the most likely candidate, since he is a descendent of Gideon Black Hand. Hence his name."

Both apprentices' jaws sagged as they gazed at the Knight. Finn spoke first. "How come you never told me?"

"Ye never asked me."

"Gideon!"

"Finn, I am only a shadow of the Black Hand, nothing more."

"Well," Mac Roth said, checking the list Gideon had given him earlier. "I tried to find any description in her manuscripts and books that might fit a blade in yer collection. Without a drawing, 'tis almost impossible." He handed the paper back to his friend.

"Now that we know Gideon probably has it, how can we tell which one it is?" asked Asher.

Mac Roth glanced down at his own notes. "According to Iona, the Spear will make its presence known on the day of the dark sun."

Finn frowned. *Dark sun? How can the sun be dark? Wait—Rafe said something about the sun and an event happening this month.* He snapped his fingers. "I think I got it." He dropped the cloth and dashed out of the kitchen. The others could hear him rummaging through the bookshelves in the living room. After a few moments, he hurried back, flipping through a thin paperback book.

"*The Farmer's Almanac?*" Asher sneered. "Going to do some gardening?"

Finn ignored him. Holding the book open for the others, he pointed to a chart. "See? A partial solar eclipse. On the tenth of July."

"Why, 'tis certain. The ancient people's way of describing that event—a dark sun." Gideon nodded at Finn. "*Gle mhaith,*" he said quietly, under his breath.

Finn grinned at his master's praise until the other boy made a gagging sound.

"So, what do we do until the eclipse?" Asher asked. He lowered the rag from his eye.

Mac Roth reached over and cupped his apprentice's chin in his palm, peering at the boy's bruises. "Ye, me lad, are going to practice keeping yer tongue in yer head." He smiled at Asher's huff of exasperation. "Remember the old Irish proverb: *Is minic a bhris béal duine a shron.*"

"Which means?" Both boys asked, at the same time.

"'Tis often that a person's mouth breaks his nose.'"

Twenty

With a screech of rusty nails, Finn pried the lid off another wooden crate. He sneezed when the dust billowed around him and dimmed the basement's single bulb. Other crates of various sizes were scattered about, most with their lids propped open or removed. "Nope, no blades in this one, either. Just junk." He pawed through layers of yellowed newspapers to the bottom. After a few more minutes of digging, he held up a long, narrow pocket of leather with a double pair of straps dangling from it. "What's this?"

Gideon glanced over his shoulder as he sorted through an oak barrel. On it, faded letters in old-fashioned script spelled out *Cripple Creek Mercantile*. "Why, that's an ankle sheath. For yer knife. Ye wear it around the calf of yer leg."

"Can I have it?"

"*May* I have it?"

"Oh, sure." Finn walked over, handing it to Gideon. "There you go."

Gideon laughed and shook his head. "Ye do that on purpose, don't ye? Just to drive me insane?"

"Totally." The corner of Finn's mouth twitched. "So, *may* I have it?"

Gideon examined it for a moment, his face thoughtful, and then tossed it back to Finn. "Of course. Wear it on yer right leg, since ye're right-handed."

Leaning over, Finn scrunched his pant leg up to his knee and strapped the sheath on the outside of his calf. "Like this?" He held the leg out to the Knight.

Gideon adjusted it, tugging it higher, then stepped back. "'Tis a useful way to keep yer blade secret, but 'tis a bit slower reaching it, in a conflict. So, be mindful of yer surroundings."

"Got it. I mean, yes, sir." Finn pulled his pant leg down and stomped his foot a few times. "It feels pretty secure. I think I'll carry it this way when I'm around Rafe." He wiped his hands on his jeans. "So can I go over there now? That was the last box."

"Help me haul these upstairs first." Gideon pointed to an assortment of weapons, some without handles, piled on the concrete floor. "Do ye think he'll want to see ye, after what happened this morning?" He scooped up most of them and made for the stairs. Finn trailed behind, trying not to drop the others.

"I hope so. I really want to apologize for Asher."

They dumped the blades on the Knight's desk, then Finn dashed upstairs. He took a minute to scrub his hands and pull on a clean tee shirt. Peering in the bathroom mirror, he grimaced at the cuts and bruises on his face. "Ye're a mess, boyo." He grinned suddenly. "But not as much a mess as Asher." He headed downstairs and paused by the front door. "I'm out of here."

"Before ye go, wash up and change shirts," Gideon called from the living room. He was hunched over the weapons scattered on the desk, examining one after another.

"Already did."

"Show me."

Finn muttered under his breath and stepped closer. "See?" He spread his arms wide.

Gideon looked up, in surprise. "The feral child is becoming civilized. I may faint."

"Ha, ha. Can I ... I mean ... *may* I go, now?"

"Have ye a weapon?"

"Oh, dang." Finn walked over to the fireplace and selected a knife from the rack. Pulling up his pant leg, he shoved it into the sheath.

"Back by four, mind ye."

Finn trotted across the street. The July sun blazed white in the sky. A cricket's trill accompanied him as he walked up the brick path to Rafe's house. Pausing under the portico, he smoothed his hair, tugged his shirt straight, then took a deep breath and rang the doorbell.

Rufus Steel answered the door. "Good heavens, Finn! What happened to you?" Stepping aside, he waved the boy in.

"Oh, I got in a..."

Before he could explain, Rafe appeared at the top of the stairs, waving both arms frantically at Finn behind his father's back. He held a finger up to his lip. *Don't say anything,* he mouthed silently as he leaned over the railing. "Hey, Finn!" he called aloud. "Come on up."

Finn nodded and started to slip around Mr. Steel, when the man stopped him with a gentle hand on his shoulder.

"Are you sure you're okay, son?"

"Yeah. I mean, yes, sir. I just...fell down."

"Fell down," the man repeated. "In your home?"

"Uh, sure."

"Were you alone?"

"N-no. Gideon was there."

"And what did he do? After you fell down?"

"Um...he gave me something to put on the bruises." *Okay, what's with all the questions?*

Finn looked up at his friend, then back at a frowning Mr. Steel. "I guess I'll go see Rafe, now." He slid out from under the man's hand and made a dash for the stairs. Without looking back, he hurried up and followed Rafe into his room.

"What was that all about?" Finn asked, shutting the door behind him.

Rafe shushed him, then motioned him over to the far side of the room. "Before I tell you," he whispered, "I need to ask you something. What's the deal with your cousin?" Rafe's black eyes bore into Finn's blue ones.

"Oh, that jerk thinks *everybody* in the world, including me, is beneath him," Finn whispered back. "He calls me *halfer* because I'm a mix of...of different people. But don't worry, I beat the crap out of him this morning, for both you and me."

"Does he look as bad as you?"

"No way. He looks a lot worse." They grinned at each other.

"Okay, here's the thing. If my dad finds out what your cousin said this morning, plus all those knives and stuff, Dad will go all protective, then we can't hang out together."

"Then, I'll just have to kick Asher's butt each time he comes over. Problem solved, and a bonus for me," Finn replied, cheerfully. After a moment, his smile faded. "So, why was your da asking me all those questions?"

Rafe flopped back on his bed, his legs dangling off the side. Clasping his hands behind his head, he stared at the ceiling. "I don't know. Dad's just nosy, I guess. Hey, want to shoot some hoops?"

"Sure." Finn leaned a hip against Rafe's desk. "But, first, I want to say I'm sorry about this morning. About what Asher said."

Rafe raised his head as he looked at Finn. "Dad always says you can't pick your relatives, just your friends." He hopped up. "Come on. I'll give you six points."

"I'll need it. I suck at basketball."

"That's for sure."

"Hey, I can't help it if I've never played before."

They raced down the stairs, each trying to trip the other, and out the front door. Finn waited under the hoop attached to the garage while Rafe retrieved the ball from behind the front hedge.

"Where's Savannah?"

"Shopping with my mom. She needed new running shoes. We're both trying out for cross country this fall, at school."

"Oh." For some reason, Finn felt disappointed by her absence. "Is that why you guys run with your da every morning? On the trails behind my house?"

Rafe nodded and passed the ball to Finn. "How can you be the only guy in America who's never played basketball before? Didn't you even play at school? A little?"

"I've never gone to school. I've been homeschooled all my life. First with my aunt and uncle in Denver, and now with Gideon."

Blowing his hair out of his eyes, Finn dribbled the ball a few times. He aimed for the basket and threw; the ball arched through the air. He groaned as it bounced off the rim with a *twang* and escaped down the driveway. Dashing after it, he scooped it out of the gutter, then turned and launched it, as hard as he could, toward the house. "Watch this. Nothing but net!"

The ball sailed over the house and landed high on the roof. It rolled down, coming to rest behind the chimney.

"You mean, nothing but roof." Rafe tilted his head back and closed his eyes in frustration. "That's my only ball."

"I'll get it." Finn hurried up the driveway.

"How are you..."

"Trust me—I got an idea. Just wait here for it."

He headed around to the side and looked up, studying the two-story house. *Okay, only a few windows on this side and I can hear Mr. Steel in the backyard. Savannah's with her mom and Rafe's out front.* He glanced at the home next door. *All clear.*

Finn held his arms out slightly, fingers spread wide, and closed his eyes. "I am a hawk on the cliff." His lips parted as the ancient power tickled the bottom of his feet, then coiled its way up his legs and along his back. "I am a hawk on the cliff," he repeated. Crouching down, he sucked in a deep breath and launched himself into the air.

He soared upward and landed with a soft thump on the shingles. Dropping to his hands and knees for balance, he kept low as he crawled up the slope toward the chimney.

"Hey, how did you get up there?"

Finn jumped. He looked down. Rafe stood near the street, oddly foreshortened as he peered up. Ignoring the question, Finn forged ahead. Reaching the ball, he leaned over and swatted it, sending it rolling down to Rafe. "Here it comes!"

As the other boy ran across the lawn in pursuit, Finn scuttled back the way he had come, sliding down to the roof's edge on his bottom. He halted, feet braced against the rain gutter.

I hate this part, he thought, looking down between his knees at the narrow strip of grass. He swallowed. *Just do it, before anyone sees you.* He eased upright and balanced on the very edge, singing softly, arms stretched like wings. *Here goes.*

He stepped off the roof, and out into thin air.

Landing with a grunt a moment later, Finn blew out his breath in relief. He glanced back up and shuddered. *I don't care what Gideon says about it getting easier—it still freaks me out.*

"Whoa! That was insane."

He spun around.

Rafe stood by the corner of the house, eyes wide and the basketball tucked under one arm. He opened and closed his mouth a few times, then finally shook his head. "Okay. How?"

"How, what?"

"Dude, how did you get up there and then jump down, without breaking a leg or something?"

"How did you think I did it?"

"Let me guess. Wings?"

"You mean, like on a bird?"

Rafe growled and threw the ball at Finn. Hard. It smacked him in the gut.

"Okay, okay, I get the message." Finn rubbed his stomach and walked over to Rafe. "I used the...um, the tree." He pointed to the tall cottonwood flanking the far corner of the house. Its limbs brushed against the bricks. "I got high enough on the trunk, then pulled myself over the rain gutter and then just wiggled onto the roof." Finn tensed as he waited. *He is* so *not buying this.*

Rafe raised his eyebrows as he stared at the tree. "Well, I guess that makes sense," he said doubtfully, scratching the back of his head. "But what about you jumping—"

"Finn?" Mr. Steel strolled from the backyard, wiping his hands on a rag. "Would you like to stay for dinner? I just got the barbeque working." He looked over at Rafe. "What do you say, son? Shall we torch some meat tonight?"

Rafe laughed. "And leave the insides all bloody, and watch Dr. Mom freak out? Sure." He turned to Finn. "Want to stay?"

"Thanks, but Gideon wants me home by four."

"Is your guardian pretty strict with you about being on time?" Mr. Steel asked, a curious expression on his kind face.

"I guess." *But not as strict as he is about holding my weapon correctly when I'm hunting goblins.*

"So will you be going to Red Rocks Middle School in the fall? With the twins?"

"No, sir. I'm homeschooled."

"I see."

Before Mr. Steel could ask another question, Finn checked his watch. "Thanks again for asking me to dinner. I better go." He nodded at Rafe. "See ya." He spun on his heels and trotted across the street, aware of their gazes on his back.

Pulling the gate securely behind him, he checked the bronze wire, then looked up at the slap of the screen door. Gideon appeared on the porch carrying a glass of iced tea in one hand.

The Knight sank down on one of the battered lawn chairs, with a contented sigh. The frame creaked as he settled back. "'Summer afternoon. The two most beautiful words in the English language,'" he quoted, offering the glass to Finn as he walked up the steps.

"Shakespeare?" Finn took a big gulp, then handed it back.

"An American. Henry James."

Finn nodded, distracted. He hoisted himself up on the porch rail, one arm looped around the post as he swung a foot. Something about Mr. Steel's questions niggled at him.

"Hey, Gideon? Why would Rafe's da ask me—?"

He froze when several crows sailed into their yard, landing with a flap and flutter of midnight wings. The birds strutted around, croaking, jerking their heads to and fro. As the De Danaan jumped to their feet, a dozen more landed on the nearby power line, jostling for position. The wire sagged under their weight.

"Get inside," Gideon shouted, over the deafening cawing. His knife flashed in his hand.

Finn bolted for the house, his master on his heels. As the Knight stopped to secure the bronze-clad door behind him, Finn raced through the house. Sliding across the kitchen floor, he kicked the back door shut, the glass panes rattling from the impact. After throwing the dead bolt, he hurried to the sink and peered out the window. Cloud shadows drifted across the yard as another storm brewed over the mountains.

Crows lined the stone wall like blackened teeth.

Finn stared, the hairs on his arms standing straight up, unable to take his gaze off the birds. After a few moments, he tore his eyes away and leaned over. Tugging up his pant leg, he slid the knife free, then straightened and looked out.

The crows had vanished.

Twenty-One

Finn whirled around as Gideon rushed into the kitchen. The Knight sighed with relief at the sight of the back door, bolted and secured.

"Did ye see anything?" Gideon took a stance next to Finn, scanning the yard. The afternoon darkened as the rainstorm approached the city.

"Just a few seconds ago, the crows were all over the place, but then they disappeared when I wasn't looking." Finn peered up at his master's profile. "Does that mean the Amandán are gone?' he asked, hopefully.

"Not bleedin' likely." Gideon gestured with his chin. "Look, ye."

Finn whipped his head around. "Oh," he breathed, eyes widening as he stared back out.

Crows fought for position along every inch of the stone wall, their sharp beaks needling each other. As Finn watched, a dozen more crash-landed into the flock. Hoarse cawing battled with the first rumble of thunder. The gloom thickened; a bolt of lightning speared the sky. Finn flinched, almost dropping his knife.

"Steady." Gideon clapped a hand on his shoulder and squeezed. "We are well protected here. Nonetheless, we'll stand vigil tonight, just to be certain." He let go and ran a thumb along the blade of his knife, as he studied Finn.

Finn nodded. "So, what do we do now?" He hoped the Knight didn't catch the faint quiver in his voice.

"The first order of business during a siege is to secure the walls or perimeters. We've done that. And now..." his voiced trailed off as he searched through a drawer. Pulling out a whetstone and a small bottle of honing oil, he handed them and his knife to Finn. "Here. Give the blade's edge a kiss."

Finn screwed up his face. "You want me to do *what?*"

Gideon laughed. "I want ye to sharpen it a bit more. Which is the second order of business." He waited, expectant.

"Make sure your weapons are ready?" At Gideon's nod, Finn dribbled a few drops of oil on the stone, smeared it around with his thumb, then began drawing the weapon across it, first one side, then the other. A rhythmic *sweesh, sweesh* filled the kitchen, muffling the sound of the falling rain.

"Flatten the angle of the blade a bit more." Gideon observed him for another moment, then went over to the refrigerator. He pulled out a platter of cold roasted chicken and a loaf of brown bread and placed them on the table, next to a basket piled with apples. After a moment's thought, he added several carrot sticks.

Continuing the task, Finn clenched his jaw at the next explosion of lightning. After the thunder faded a few seconds later, he glanced out the window and cleared his throat. "Looks like the birds have taken off again," he said, trying to sound nonchalant.

"Aye, they may do that from time to time, depending on the Amandán's location, back there in the woods."

"Is it normal for them to surround a house like this?" He laid the whet stone on the counter and wiped the blade on a clean cloth.

Gideon hesitated for a moment, then spoke softly. "No, boyo, it is not." He finished setting out the impromptu supper and turned to face the apprentice. "I'll tell ye the truth of it—I'm not sure what the beasties are up to." He walked over and took the weapon back. Grunting with satisfaction, he put it away, then gestured toward the table. "We should eat whilst we can. It may be a longish night."

Gideon shifted his weight to his other leg as he stood watch in the darkened kitchen. Dragging a hand down his face, he grimaced at the stubble along his jaw. *Perhaps I should grow a beard again. T'would save time shaving, to be sure. Why, I haven't worn one since...*

He shoved the rest of the thought away and kicked it back into the corner of his heart. Clamping down on his memories with an iron will, he glanced through the window to scan the yard for the thousandth time. He frowned when a single crow appeared, almost invisible in the inky night. It flapped awkwardly, with soaked wings, before landing on the wall.

"Finn," he called over a shoulder. "It appears the beasties are drawing near again." At the lack of response, he turned and hurried through the shadowy house to the living room.

A figure sat slumped on the wide sill, silhouetted against the front window. A whuffling sound echoed through the silent room.

Fast asleep, I'll warrant, Gideon thought. *Well, I cannot expect an old head on young shoulders. I best wake him, though.*

With the stealth of a hunting wolf, he edged around the furniture and eased closer. Narrowing his eyes, he peered into his apprentice's sleeping face pressed against the glass. A line of drool slid from the corner of Finn's mouth and trickled down the pane. A knife was loosely clasped in one hand.

A snort of laughter escaped the Knight.

At the sound, Finn lurched to his feet, then stumbled, wind-milling his arms for balance. As he fell backwards, the tip of his knife snagged the curtain next to him. With a cry, Finn crashed to the floor. A moment later, the drape followed in a puff of dust, the drapery rod a second after that. It whacked him on the head with a sharp crack.

"They're in the house," Finn shouted, his voice muffled by yards of fabric. He began kicking frantically.

Dodging the flailing feet, Gideon peeled the curtain off his apprentice. Once Finn emerged, the Knight took a step back and tried to quell his laughter. He failed.

"It's not funny." Finn shoved the rest of the material to one side and scrambled to his feet. He glared up at the Knight before retrieving his blade from under the pile. "What are you doing, sneaking up on me like that and then growling in my face? You're lucky I didn't knife you."

"Aye, that I am." Gideon waved a hand in dismissal when Finn started to pick up the drapery and rod. "Leave those for now. We need to reconnoiter a bit, outside."

"Are the crows back?"

"Only one, as yet." Gideon led the way to the kitchen door. He peered out, then slid the bolt, slowly and silently, and inched the door open. "Behind me, now," he whispered. "And instant obedience if I order ye to retreat. Understand?"

"Yes, sir."

Gideon swung the door further ajar and stepped out into the night.

The stars winked in and out of view as the last of the storm clouds drifted away. Rain-soaked pines perfumed the air. The solitary crow fluttered its wings, then stilled.

Signaling Finn to wait, Gideon stalked further into the yard and paused by the picnic table. He cocked his head to listen for a moment, then motioned for Finn to come along.

Knife at the ready, he joined the Knight. Together, they crept toward the stone wall; Finn winced with each step as his shoes squelched in the sodden grass.

When the De Danaan reached the center of the yard, the crow opened its beak. Master and apprentice froze. The bird closed its beak again.

"Make up yer bleedin' mind, ye manky bird," Gideon said, under his breath. He relaxed when the bird heaved itself into the night and flapped away. "Stay here, Finn." He walked toward the far edge of the yard, his knife gleaming softly in the starlight. Reaching the wall, he paused, then leaned over it.

Finn gasped as Gideon hoisted himself up on the wall and swung a leg over. Before he could move, the Knight disappeared on the other side. Twigs snapped and leaves rustled as he tracked back and forth, then the noise ceased. Silence filled the night.

"Gideon?" Finn whispered. On shaky legs, he crept forward; the woods beyond seemed crammed with goblin-shaped shadows. His pulse hammered in his ears. Reaching the wall, he laid his palm hesitantly along the top.

A hand reached out of the darkness and grabbed his wrist.

Finn yelped and swung his knife. It was deflected with a clang and a twist, sending a shower of sparks into the air. Gideon's grinning face appeared a moment later. He let go of Finn's arm and jumped back over the wall, landing next to the apprentice.

"Now, I'll place a fair bet that ye just wet yer trousers."

The Journal of Finnegan MacCullen: July 2

What I Learned ~~Today~~ Yesterday:

Man, am I tired. We were up all night, but nothing ever happened.

Between all the stuff about the Spear, the fight with Asher, Rafe catching me doing my De Danaan thing, and the Amandán trying to get us all night, I don't know where to start.

I can't even think what I really learned. Except that Gideon thinks it's funny to scare the piss out of me.

Literally. (I just didn't tell him that.)

Twenty-Two

"And, with yer own knee," Gideon said, trying to control a smile as he crouched down on the front lawn next to Finn. He held a handkerchief to Finn's injured nose, the apprentice's blood already smeared across his knuckles. "'Tis a pity. Yer bruises were just starting to fade from the fight with Asher two days ago, too." His lips twitched as he readjusted the cloth; his morning mug of tea sat abandoned on the edge of their porch.

"Stop laughing at me. It hurts!" Finn leaned back on his hands, legs stuck out in front of him. He tilted his head forward as Gideon pinched gently. "I feel so stupid," he said, voice muffled by the Knight's hand.

"And why is that? Any apprentice could knock himself in the face with his knee whilst demonstrating a back flip off the porch. It's perfectly normal."

"Really? Did your other apprentice ever do it?"

"Well, no."

Finn rolled his eyes.

After a few minutes, the Knight pulled the cloth away. "The gush has slowed to a trickle." He ran a bloodstained finger along the bridge of Finn's nose. "I don't believe it's broken." Wiping his hands clean as best he could, he rose and grabbed Finn under the arm and hauled him to his feet. "Up ye get. Take a seat and I'll fetch yet another poultice for ye. We might need to plant a second hedge of the *slainte* nettle, at this rate."

"That's *so* not funny."

As Gideon disappeared inside the house, Finn walked over and sank down on the middle step. He wiggled his nose gingerly and winced. *I'm glad Rafe didn't see that.*

A movement across the street caught his eyes. "Son of a goat," he whispered, watching as Mr. Steel and Rafe strolled toward him.

"Hey, Finn," Rafe called as they reached the gate. "We were just—holy moly, what happened?" He gazed wide-eyed at the blood drying on Finn's upper lip and chin.

Finn grinned sheepishly. "Oh, I was trying to show Gideon how I can do this move off the top step and I hit myself in the face with my knee." He shook his head. "Talk about a klutz," he said as they pushed through the gate and walked up to the porch.

Mr. Steel frowned; his lips pressed into a thin line. He began to say something, but Gideon stepped out, a damp cloth in either hand. One was stained a dark greenish brown.

"Good morning, Rufus. Rafe." Gideon nodded politely, then handed the stained cloth down to Finn. "Hold it on for at least ten minutes, lad." Turning to the Steels, he asked, "Did he tell ye what happened?" His blue eyes twinkled.

"He did." Rufus Steel stared back, eying the blood on Gideon's knuckles. "It seems a bit farfetched."

"Oh, ye don't know the boyo. He can injure himself sitting in a chair, reading."

"Hey! I'm not *that* clumsy!" Finn peered up at the Knight, his face partially obscured by the cloth.

"Actually, ye are," Gideon said.

"I came over to ask if Finn would be able to collect our mail and newspapers for the next week," Mr. Steel said. "We're going camping over the Fourth of July holiday." He studied Finn, his face thoughtful. "We'll pay you, of course."

"No problem. And you don't need to pay me, Mr. Steel. I want to help."

"Well, I appreciate it. We'll be back on the sixth." He gazed at Finn for another moment. "Unless you would like to come with us? I know it's short notice, but—"

"No, we've plans of our own, but many thanks," Gideon interrupted.

"I see." Mr. Steel started to speak, then stopped. "Perhaps another time. Well, come on, Rafe. Better go load up the car. Thanks again, Finn." With a nod, he headed back across the street.

"Camping. With my family," Rafe said, making a face. "Kill me now." He trudged away with a wave of his hand.

"So what *are* we doing for the holiday?" Finn took the clean, damp cloth Gideon handed him and wiped his face. "Did I get all the blood?"

Plucking the washcloth from the boy's hand, Gideon swiped at a few missed streaks, then tossed it to one side. "There's a pack of troublesome Amandán several miles back in the hills west of here. I thought we might do a bit of hunting tomorrow night—"

"Yes!" Finn pumped his fist into the air.

"—with Mac Roth and Asher."

"No!"

Green stars burst in the night sky over the tree tops. The fireworks tinted the faces of the four De Danaan with a mossy light as they made their way through the woods. Purple and red and blue flashes followed. The thunder of the neighborhood fireworks show was magnified by the hills.

"Now, do ye see why this is such a splendid night to hunt?" Mac Roth spoke over his shoulder to the two apprentices following him.

Gideon stalked a few yards behind the party as rear guard. "The noise and activity covers up anything we do, while the fireworks confuse the beasties."

"I sure hope so," Finn said. He dug in his pocket for his moonstone as they hiked along the narrow trail. In tugging the stone free, his elbow caught Asher in the ribs.

Asher stumbled. "Hey, watch it!" He shoved back.

Finn staggered sideways, dropping the stone. "You son of a goat." He squatted down, patting the ground as he attempted to locate the rock.

Looking down at Finn, Asher smirked. "Oops."

Gideon appeared behind the boys. "Finn, what are ye doing?"

"I dropped my moonstone." He ran his hands over the rocky trail, trying to find it by touch. *I knew I should have left it at home,* he thought. *It's not like it works or anything.* Scooping up handfuls of pebbles, he held them close to his face, hoping to spot the familiar shape. *Crap, I'll never find it in the dark.* Dismay flooded him.

Gideon crouched down beside him. "Let me help." He dragged his fingers slowly over the area, until a pale light flickered by his left hand. He stilled his movement. A milky radiance swelled under his palm. "Success," he said. Picking up the moonstone, he handed it to Finn. It winked out as he released it. "Carrying it for luck, eh?" Gideon said, in an undertone.

Finn nodded. He stood up and ran a thumb across it, then tucked it back into his deepest pocket. Before Gideon could stop him, he marched over to Asher and crowded him, chest to chest. "You always got to be a jerk?"

"What's the big deal? They're easy enough to find," Asher replied, standing his ground. "Oh. Wait. That's right. Moonstones don't light for halfers. Only real De Danaan."

Finn pointed to his torc. "I'm more De Danaan than you'll ever be."

Mac Roth stepped out of the darkness. They both yelped when heavy hands clamped down on the scruffs of their necks.

"Keep it up, lads, and I'll feed the pair of ye to the first Amandán I can invite to supper," Mac Roth growled, shaking them roughly. He let go, cuffing first Asher, then Finn, with equal force, nearly knocking them off their feet. "Asher. Up front with me." He continued along the trail, his apprentice on his heels.

Ears ringing, Finn fell in beside an amused Gideon. He took a deep breath, then another, counting silently to ten. *Ye gods, he hits hard.*

Watching Mac Roth drape a thick arm across Asher's shoulder as he spoke to his apprentice, Finn shook his head. "I don't see how a Knight like Mac Roth can stand being around someone like Ass-her. I mean, Asher."

The corner of Gideon's mouth quirked. "And there be the kettle calling the pot black."

"What the heck does that mean?"

"Finn, ye're not perfect yerself. And the expression means ye mustn't criticize someone for doing things you do. Ye have yer moments, just as Asher does."

"You mean, like my temper?"

"Aye, like yer temper. And stubbornness. Yer less than stellar table manners. And—"

"Okay—I get it already," He peeked at his master out of the corner of his eye. "So, are you sorry you took me on as your apprentice?"

Gideon scanned the woods before answering. "I am. Ye've been a pain in the arse since the very first day. I only keep ye around for the free labor."

"Hey!"

With a chuckle, he glanced over. "Explain something to me, boyo. Why does it bother ye so when Asher taunts ye about being half mortal, yet ye've a good friend who's human?" He looked up, as another rocket exploded over the hills. "Are ye ashamed of yer mother?"

"What? No! It's just the way Asher says it. Like I'm dirt."

"Finnegan MacCullen, 'twill always be Tuatha De Danaan who will look down on ye for being part mortal. Just as there are humans who will look down on Rafe for being black. Savannah for being a female. Meself for being a foreigner. Even ye and I because of our lack of money. Such is the nature of this round world."

"Yeah, and it sucks."

"Aye, it does. I should teach ye to say that in Gaelic." He started to add something, then froze. "Mac Roth," he called, in warning.

"Aye, I heard them, Lir."

Gideon and Finn slipped forward on silent feet and joined the other two De Danaan at the foot of a towering outcropping of rock. The trail wound through a small clearing at the cliff's base.

Pushing Finn and Asher closer to the rock, Gideon stood in the middle of the clearing, head cocked as he listened. Mac Roth edged further up the path, his bulk punishing the vegetation as he cast about. *They're like a wolf and a bear*, Finn thought, as he watched the two Knights.

After a few minutes, Mac Roth returned. "Gideon, there's only a couple of the beasties, about halfway down the hill. We'll split up and circle around. Attack them in the classic hammer and anvil move."

"Finally—some action." Asher said with glee. He tossed his knife into the air with a flip of a wrist and caught it by its handle. He started to join his master, when Mac Roth stopped him.

"Asher, I want ye to remain here. This rock face will give ye some protection."

"Oh, come on, Mac Roth." Asher spread his arms wide. "I can do this."

"Not this time, boyo." He caught his apprentice by the arm before he could storm off in frustration. "Now, lad," he said softly. He waited until Asher looked up at him. "Ye know how delicate I am, and how 'twould break me heart if something happened to ye. I'll not have ye getting killed in front of me old friend. Just think how embarrassed I would be."

Asher sighed and looked down, scuffing the dirt with the toe of his shoe. "Please? Please, let me go with you?" he whispered.

Mac Roth placed his huge paw on Asher's head. "No." He pushed the boy back toward the outcropping, ignoring the rest of his pleas. "Stay here. And I want yer moonstone out, and in use."

I don't like the guy, Finn thought as he watched, *but I know how he feels. I'm sure glad I get to go, though.* Tightening his grip on his weapon, he walked over to Gideon. "Okay, I'm all set."

"And just what do ye think ye're doing?"

"I'm...I'm going with you."

Gideon shook his head and pointed toward the other apprentice. "No, ye are not. I want ye guarding Asher's back. And vice versa."

Disbelief nailed Finn's feet in place. "But, that's not fair. I've earned my torc—I have a right to hunt with you!" His voice cracked in frustration.

"This isn't a bleedin' democracy," Gideon growled back. "The only rights ye have are the ones I give ye. And tonight, I am giving ye the right to stay alive. Now, get yer arse over by that rock."

Body rigid, Finn stomped over to Asher. He took a stance a few yards away from the other boy. Scowling, he muttered something under his breath, just low enough to avoid his master's wrath.

Gideon turned away, fighting a smile. He nodded at Mac Roth. They eased through the undergrowth surrounding the clearing, and disappeared into the darkness.

Twenty-Three

Finn blew out a long breath. His anger at being left behind drained away as he listened to the fading rustle of the departing Knights. He shifted from foot to foot as the woods grew silent.

Looking around, he noticed the remains of an old campfire, tucked back in a slight depression at the foot of the outcropping. *I guess this is a popular place.* He took a few steps away and glanced up at the rock towering over his head. As he watched, a barrage of fireworks exploded in a grand finale, then faded away. *Well, at least they can't ambush us from behind,* he thought as he craned his neck, trying to gauge the rock's height.

"Nervous?" Asher said with a sneer in his voice. Without waiting for an answer, he hurled his knife across the clearing and buried its point deep in a sapling. The tree shuddered from the impact; a few leaves fluttered down.

"No. Why—are you?" Finn watched as Asher walked over and yanked the weapon free. "Is that why you keep messing around with your knife?"

"Just keeping my skills up. I might have to save your sorry butt tonight."

Finn snorted. "Right. That's why the Knights left you in my care. I should get paid for all the baby-sitting I'm doing." He studied the edge of his weapon. "I could buy a..." he began, then froze.

Branches snapped in the bushes at the far side of the clearing. As both apprentices stared wide-eyed into the night, a hulking figure rose from the center of the thicket. Its thick body was half-hidden in the underbrush. It swayed from foot to foot as if studying them, and then turned and crashed away, vanishing into a stand of pines. The lower branches waved wildly for a moment, then stilled.

Finn tensed. He tried to remember to breathe as he backed toward the cliff, his gut squirming and the knife held out in front of him. His eyes darted from shadow to shadow. Gravel rattled. He jerked his head around and stared down the trail, eyeing the far bend.

The path was empty.

"Finn."

He whirled around at Asher's whisper. The other apprentice pointed toward the opposite side of the clearing. Finn nodded and eased over, matching Asher's cautious movements, as both boys pressed themselves against the rock wall. Standing side by side, they glanced at each other.

"Now, I get to see if you're really that good." Asher fished in his pocket for the moonstone. He held it up. Light welled out from between his fingers. "Here, kitty, kitty," he called.

In spite of himself, Finn laughed. Asher grinned back reluctantly, his sandy hair almost white in the moonstone's glow. Swinging his arm, he scanned the area. The beam darted from one shape to another, from tree to boulder to bush.

They jumped when the light caught a pair of eyes glowing neon green, like a cat's. The eyes seemed to float, bodiless, in the shadow of an ancient pine tree. Finn cursed when the eyes blinked and disappeared. Asher held the stone higher, widening the search. As branches cracked off to their right, faint laughter jerked their heads to the left.

"There's two," Finn whispered.

"Or more." Asher swallowed, his throat making a clicking sound. "Um ... maybe we should find the Knights. Let them know where all the action is."

"No way! Gideon'll kill me if I leave this spot."

"Yeah, I suppose you're right." Asher shook his head. "I'd rather face a whole pack of Amandán than Mac Roth when he's pissed off."

Finn nodded as he squinted into the dark, grateful to be talking. To keep the fear at bay. "When Gideon is really mad, his accent gets so thick I can't understand him," he joked, trying to keep his voice steady. "Once, when he was yelling at me for something, I thought he said to get him a broom. So, I did, and then he got even madder because he thought I was making fun of him." Even as he spoke, Finn swiveled his head from side to side. He tightened his leg muscles to keep them from shaking.

"What did he really say?"

"'Get to yer room.'" Finn shrugged. "Who knew?"

Their heads jerked up at the sudden *kaw-kaw* from overhead. Black shapes wheeled against the stars, blotting out the points of light.

With a roar, the goblin burst out the bushes in front of them. It barreled into them and knocked them aside like bowling pins. The boys tumbled apart. Asher's stone flew out of his hand and plunged the area into darkness.

"*Poc sídhe*," the Amandán screeched, as it skidded to a halt. It swung around toward Finn.

A sour stench filled Finn's nostrils as the creature closed on him—it scrabbled for his face with black-tipped fingers. Dodging to one side, Finn twisted under the goblin's reach. "I am a spear on the attack, pouring forth combat," he shouted. With a grunt, he thrust his blade into its side.

Letting go of the handle, he jumped back and squeezed his eyes tight. Powder coated his face. "Oh, gross!" He spat, trying to clear his mouth. "Man, they taste just like feet smell." He blinked and wiped his watering eyes, then picked up the blade. "You okay?"

Asher nodded, scrambling to his feet. "Yeah, thanks." He bent over and ran the fingertips of one hand back and forth across the ground; the other hand clutched his knife. He worked his way further from the rock to the edge of the clearing. After a few minutes, both boys breathed sighs of relief when the light blazed under Asher's palm. With a cry of triumph, Asher turned around and held it up.

As the beam flickered over Finn, Asher gasped. "Duck!"

Finn flung himself down as Asher's knife whistled over his head like a flash of bronze lightning. It flipped twice, end over end, before burying itself hilt-deep in the chest of the Amandán creeping up behind Finn. The beast exploded, coating Finn for the second time and dusting the rock wall. The blade fell to the ground with a metallic *clink*.

Raising his head, Finn squinted into the light streaming from Asher's stone. "Wow," he breathed, still sprawled on the ground. "Nice throw!" They looked at each other for a minute. Asher's growing smile matched Finn's.

At that moment, a pair of thick, hairy arms shot from the darkness and grabbed Asher from behind, jerking the boy off his feet. The stone tumbled from his hand, its light winking out.

Asher's scream split the night.

Finn scrambled to his feet and tore across the clearing. "Let him go!" He slashed at the retreating form.

With a roar, it whirled around, dropping the limp figure as it faced the new threat. Asher lay crumpled on his side, a boneless heap at the Amandán's feet. The goblin laughed as it sized up Finn. "*Nar*, yer nothing but a whelp."

Finn glanced down at Asher, then raised his head. Narrowing his eyes, he gripped his knife. "And you're an ugly git," he said hoarsely. Before the goblin could move, he charged.

Ducking under the swinging arms, he dropped to one knee. The stink of the monster's hide burned his nostrils. Shouting the Song, he thrust upward and buried the blade to the hilt. With a screech, the beast exploded.

140

Finn flung himself backwards. Rolling to his feet, he snatched the weapon from the pile of remains. Sprinting over to Asher, he fell to his knees beside him.

He's just hurt, he thought, his heart punishing his ribs like a crazed boxer. *That's all—he's just unconscious.* He reached out with numb fingers, then hesitated, afraid to turn him over.

Sucking in an unsteady breath, he placed a hand on Asher's shoulder and pulled. The boy flopped over like a rag doll. His pale face was relaxed, as if he were asleep.

Finn sank back onto his bottom. He stared at Asher's chest, willing it to rise and fall. *Maybe if I keep watching, he'll start breathing again.* Pulling his knees up to his chest, he wrapped his arms around them, his gaze locked on Asher.

After a moment, he began shaking.

Twenty-Four

"Odd for them to have kept fleeing from us." Gideon picked his way around the heavy underbrush. He led the way back up the hill.

Mac Roth swung his dagger like a machete, clearing small bushes from his path as he stomped along behind the other Knight. "Cowardly beasties. We should've brought the lads along after all. With the four of us, we could've cornered them and allowed Asher to bag his first one." He smacked another branch aside. "He's been in a fever to earn the torc, ever since Finn won his."

"Well, I hope we find those two firebrands still alive after leaving them alone without a referee." Gideon craned his neck as he continued up the slope toward the outcropping. They hiked along in silence for a few minutes, both relaxing at their first glimpse of the cliff silhouetted against the stars.

"'Tis certainly quiet up there," Gideon said after a moment, a look of unease growing on his face.

"Aye. And dark, too."

Without another word, they broke into a sprint.

Finn's teeth chattered as the shaking grew worse. He found himself missing Gideon's presence so badly he ached. Hugging his knees tighter, he tried to stop trembling as he kept his gaze fixed on Asher. The scene looped through his head over and over: the look of terror on the other boy's face as the Amandán yanked him back, his shrill cry, and the way it had so abruptly ended.

It's my fault. He died because of me. I should've gone with him to find his stone, since he didn't have a weapon. I should have been guarding his back. It's my fault. He wiped his face on his shoulder, leaving a damp smear on the tee shirt sleeve.

A growing horror twisted his heart. "Oh, gods," he whispered, eyes widening in shock. "It was *me*. I made this happen." *I let him get killed because I didn't like him. I told Gideon that I wished Asher was dead. And now he is!*

He froze as two figures crashed through the bushes behind him and into the clearing.

Lurching to his feet, Finn stumbled away from Asher's body. He spun around and swung his weapon as one of them charged toward him. Sparks shot upward as a blade parried his knife with a clang and sent it spinning out of his hand. The figure reached out of the dark for him, speaking his name.

"Finn—it's me, boyo."

He blinked. "G-Gideon?"

The Knight nodded, then stepped closer. His eyes swept up and down. "Are ye hurt?" he asked, taking the boy's arm.

He shook his head, unable to speak around the lump in his throat. They both turned at the moan of anguish behind them.

Mac Roth knelt on the ground, Asher's lifeless body sagging in his arms. For a moment, the Knight gazed at the boy's white face. "Oh, lad," he whispered. Tears trickled down his cheeks and soaked his beard. Without taking his eyes off his apprentice, he spoke over his shoulder. "And Finn?"

"Aye, he's fine. Just shaken up." Gideon looked around the clearing, noting the ashy residue covering the cliff and the ground, as well as both boys. "How many were there?"

Finn hesitated for a moment, then held up three fingers.

"Ye gods," the Knight muttered. He cleared his throat, and then stepped over to his friend, still crouched on the ground.

"Let me carry him for ye."

Shaking his head, Mac Roth rose to his feet. His bulk dwarfed the boy as he cradled Asher in his arms. "Thank ye, but no. I'll take the wee one." Without another word, he started down the trail with his burden.

Gideon watched for a moment, then tore his eyes away. As Finn stood motionless in the center of the clearing, the Knight surveyed the area. His light swept about as he collected weapons and located Asher's moonstone, which he tucked in his pocket. "We best keep mine out, though. Just in case, eh?"

Finn nodded absently.

Gideon sighed. "Come, lad. Let's go home."

Twenty-Five

Standing next to his master on the isolated hilltop, Finn glanced around as other De Danaan made their way through the woods to the burial site. Tall torches, planted at the four corners, guarded the grave, their flames almost invisible in the bright afternoon light. A small figure, shrouded in white, rested on an emerald cloth next to the grave. Nearby, a mound of dirt sat next to a pile of stones. The smell of freshly dug earth made Finn queasy.

Stillness fell over the mourners as the last ones arrived and took their places. Asher's family wept softly as they laid gifts of food in the grave for their youngest son, murmuring the traditional farewell. Their words were drowned out by the snap and hiss of torch flames.

When they were finished, Mac Roth stepped forward. Shrugging out of his leather jacket, he knelt down and draped it over Asher's form. "To keep ye warm on yer long journey to the Otherworld." He rested a hand on the boy's covered head for a moment, then stood and took a stance at the foot of the grave.

Gideon followed. Slipping a knife from his belt, he tucked it into a fold of the burial shroud next to the young De Danaan's right side.

"To protect ye on yer long journey to the Otherworld." He patted Asher's arm. "Thank ye," he added, then rejoined Finn.

His eyes gritty from lack of sleep, Finn gazed at Asher for a moment. He reached up, loosened the torc from around his neck, and pulled it off. Walking on wooden legs, he approached the form. "To wear when you reach the Otherworld." He leaned over and laid the golden circle on Asher's chest. "You totally nailed that goblin."

Stepping back, he watched as two other Tuatha De Danaan lifted Asher by the four corners of the cloth. Kneeling, they lowered him into the grave, then flipped the fabric over to envelop him in green. Taking up shovels, they quickly filled the hole.

Once it was done, the rest of Tuatha De Danaan began stacking rocks, one by one, on the raw dirt. Slowly, a mound rose. When they finished the cairn, Gideon stepped over to Mac Roth.

"Here. Ye'll want this." He pressed Asher's glowing moonstone into his grieving friend's hand.

Mac Roth gazed down at the stone, lost in his large paw. With a sigh, he laid it at the foot of the site. "To illuminate yer steps on yer long journey to the Otherworld."

For a long minute, the moonstone continued to blaze, its light brilliant in the afternoon sun. Then, it faded.

"Eat yer supper, boyo."

Finn blinked and looked up from his seat at the kitchen table. "I-I'm sorry, what?"

"'Tis getting cold." Gideon nodded toward the bowl in front of Finn.

Trying to forget the images of Asher's last moments, Finn picked up his spoon. He poked at the thick lentil soup. Chunks of cabbage floated to the surface. The vegetable's greenish color reminded him of the pelt of the Amandán. He pushed it away. "I'm not hungry. Can

I be excused?" Without waiting for an answer, he rose and carried the dish to the sink.

Leaving the kitchen, he wandered into the living room and flopped down on one end of the sofa, the worn leather creaking under him. He half-listened to the sounds of Gideon washing up. *I should go help*, he thought, slouching lower on the cushions and swinging his feet up. Resting his head on the arm of the sofa, he gazed across the room at the weapon collection. A numbness, more of heart than of limb, weighed him down.

Gideon sauntered in from the kitchen and headed over to the fireplace. Removing his knife from his belt, he placed it on the rack in its customary spot before joining Finn.

"And just what are these doing on the furniture?" he asked. He picked up Finn's feet, and tugged off one shoe, then the other, before tossing them in the corner. "Shove along." When Finn scrunched his legs up, Gideon sank down on the other end of the sofa. For several minutes, they sat together in silence; the long summer dusk softened the room.

"T'was a gracious gesture, giving Asher yer torc."

"He earned it last night. He saved my life."

"Aye, that he did." Gideon glanced over at Finn, noting the dark circles under the boy's eyes. "To bed with ye now."

"I'm not tired yet." Finn picked at a rip in the knee of his jeans. "Can I just stay here for awhile longer?"

Gideon started to speak, and then nodded. He patted Finn's foot, then rose and went to his desk. He gathered up his journal and a pen before returning to his seat. Flipping open the canvas-covered ledger, he turned a few pages and began. The scratch of his pen whispered around the room.

"Gideon?"

"Finn."

It's my fault, Gideon. Asher got killed because of me. I wished him dead. And now he is. And I can't ever take it back. "Um...oh, nothing."

For a long while, he listened to the sound of his master writing. It was a comfort in some strange way. Stretching his arms over his head, he stared up at the ceiling and let his eyelids slide shut.

Pen motionless in his hand, Gideon sat gazing at his sleeping apprentice's face. "*Codladh sumh*, lad," he whispered.

The Journal of Gideon Lir: July 5

The sorrow is deeper when a young one falls in battle. I grieve for the O'Neill family and for Mac Roth. For all Tuatha De Danaan who have lost a loved one in our long war against the Amandán.

We are a warrior people and accept death as a part of life's circle.

But I am grateful to the gods beyond measure that Finnegan is still alive.

Twenty-Six

Finn scowled at the knock on the front door. "Go away," he grumbled. Grabbing the remote beside him, he punched up the volume on the television. The room was dark, with the drapes pulled closed against the midmorning sun. A second knock came, louder this time.

"Finnegan," Gideon yelled from upstairs. "Get the bleedin' door!"

With a growl, he pushed off the sofa and marched over. Yanking the door open, he squinted against the daylight. "Hi, Rafe," he said, scratching his stomach through his tee shirt. "When did you get back?"

"Last night. Talk about boring." Rafe waited on the threshold, staring at Finn's face. "Are you sick? You don't look so good."

"Been busy the last couple of days." *Yeah, busy getting another apprentice killed.* "So, what do you want?"

Rafe's eyes widened at Finn's blunt tone. "I just came over to see if you wanted to do something, and to get our mail and newspapers."

Grabbing the stack of papers and letters stored in the crate, Finn handed them to Rafe. "Nah, I'm good."

Rafe hesitated for a moment, waiting for a reason. Finn stared back.

"Anything else?"

"I guess not." Without another word, Rafe spun around and left.

Finn swung the door shut with a thump and walked back into the living room. Flinging himself down on the couch, he stared at the television screen. *Nice job—brushing off your friend like that.*

"Who was that?" Gideon asked as he clumped downstairs, his workman boots beating the wooden treads.

"Just Rafe. He came by to get their stuff."

"And ye dinna wish to spend some time with him?"

"Not really." Finn glanced up as Gideon stalked past and turned off the television.

"Well, then. On yer feet, boyo." The Knight walked over to the rack and gathered a dozen knives. "Target practice, this morning."

"Can I skip training this morning? I feel lousy."

"No. Get yer shoes on, and meet me in the back yard." Gideon hefted the weapons in his arms and left. The back screen door slapped closed a moment later.

He's making me do target practice because of what happened, Finn thought as he pulled his sneakers on and headed outside. *Like it'll do Asher any good, now.* He dragged his feet across the lawn to join his master at the far corner of the yard.

Gideon placed the knives in a row along the top of the stone wall. Picking up the first one, he handed it to Finn. "Keep yer arm loose and fluid. Remember to follow through." He stepped back, and nodded toward the target attached to the side of the house.

After five attempts, Finn gave up. Knives lay scattered on the ground below the target, except for the one he'd managed to stick into the house.

"Maybe ye need a larger target?" Gideon suggested.

Maybe you need to shut up, Finn thought. He trudged over and picked up the weapons. Gideon joined him, studying the wood siding.

"Hmm. We've quite a collection of holes." He poked a finger into the largest one. "I may need to move the target to a less vulnerable location. But, in the meantime, we'd best replace this board." He took the blades from Finn. "Go get the rest of the knives and put them away. Then, we'll take a drive to the lumber yard for some siding."

Finn made a face. "Do I *have* to go?"

Gideon ignored him. "I want ye in the truck in five minutes. And make sure ye're armed."

Whatever, Finn thought as Gideon went inside. *Like it matters anymore.*

Sitting on the trunk's open tailgate, Finn stared into the distance, lost in thought. The lumber yard's loading bay was deserted in the noontime heat. Grasshoppers danced about with loud *brrr-cheeps* in the empty, weed-covered lot bordering the yard.

I should have gotten up right away, he thought. *After Asher threw his knife. I could have gotten to him in time, if I had been on my feet.* He squeezed his eyes shut, trying to block out the video in his head. It played over and over, showing Asher's face when the beast grabbed him.

A dull clank made him open his eyes. As he watched, a worker in a hardhat crawled out from beneath the flight of metal steps leading to the warehouse's back door. Frowning, Finn watched for a moment, then shrugged. With a sigh, he slumped forward again, his elbows resting on his knees as he bowed his head.

Asher's scream echoed in his mind.

He slapped his hands over his ears, humming tunelessly as he tried to block out the memory. A shadow flickered on the edge of his vision. Hands still cupped on either side of his head, he looked behind him.

A crow perched on the wall of the truck bed, its beak open in a silent caw as it bobbed its head. Finn dropped his arms. The hairs on the back of his neck stiffened at an odd sound. He turned back.

The workman stood a few feet away, his face blank as he stared at Finn. Then he smiled, his teeth large and square and yellow.

Scrambling to his feet, Finn backed toward the cab. His fingers clawed at his pant leg as he went for a knife.

His leg was bare.

"Oooh, crap," Finn breathed. He backed up further. In desperation, he crawled up on the roof of the cab, stomach knotting with fear. His eyes widened as the man clambered onto the tailgate. As Finn watched, the man's features began twisting and stretching. A stench, like week-old roadkill, filled the air. With a final wet pop, the creature finished transforming.

"Where's yer little friends—too scared to come play, eh?" it snarled. "*Bah*, we'll hunt them down, soon enough. Give them a taste of what happens to humans who joins up with ye De Danaan." The Amandán stalked toward him. The truck rocked from side to side with the creature's rolling gait. Finn was prepared to jump as it stretched out black-tipped fingers, as if inviting the boy into its arms.

"Heads up, ye manky beast!" roared a voice.

The goblin whirled around.

Gideon swung the short length of wooden siding like a Louisville Slugger. With a hollow thud, he hit the Amandán on the side of the head. It tumbled out, over the side of the truck bed.

"Get in!" Gideon tossed the board into the truck and dashed for the cab.

Finn slid down the windshield and rolled off the hood. Yanking open the door, he jumped inside as Gideon gunned the engine and hit the gas. The truck fish-tailed as it roared around the corner of the warehouse.

The Knight slowed when he reached the parking lot. He glanced in the rearview mirror while he wove his way between parked cars. Turning out of the lot and onto the main road, he headed home.

"Are ye all right?"

Finn nodded and wiped the sweat from his forehead. He tucked his shaking hands under his legs, so Gideon wouldn't notice. They drove in silence for a few minutes. Finn kept his eyes fixed straight ahead, dreading what was coming next. *Maybe he didn't notice I was unarmed.*

No such luck. Irish or otherwise.

"And just where was yer weapon?"

Finn swallowed. "I forgot it."

"Sorry, what did ye say?"

"I said, 'I forgot it'," Finn repeated, louder. He tensed his shoulders.

Gideon slammed his hand on the steering wheel. "Ye forgot it? Finnegan MacCullen, we are in the middle of a bleedin' war!"

"I know, but ..."

"The Amandán are everywhere. In the largest numbers we've ever seen!"

"I know, but ..."

"Asher perished not three days ago, and ye forget yer bleedin' weapon?!"

Anger and guilt flared up inside of him. "Yeah, I forgot it, okay? I screwed up," he yelled back. "Just like I screwed up with Asher!"

At that moment, Gideon braked for a red light. With a curse, Finn threw the door open and jumped out. Dashing for the sidewalk, he took off, running. As his master shouted for him to stop, he pelted down a side street, tears blurring his vision.

Twenty-Seven

Forty-five minutes later, Finn walked up the path to Rafe's front door. Swallowing through a dry mouth, he pushed his damp hair off his forehead, hesitated, then pressed the doorbell. As he waited, he glanced over a shoulder at his own empty driveway. *Gideon's probably still driving around looking for me. Good. Gives him something to do besides yell at me all the time.*

The door opened.

"Hey, Rafe."

"Hi," Rafe replied, his expression guarded. For a moment, neither of them spoke as they stared at each other.

Finn looked away first. "Um...do you still want to do something?"

"Nah, I'm kind of busy." He shut the door before Finn could say anything else.

Staring at the closed door, Finn nodded. *Well, I guess I deserved that,* he thought. He turned and made his way across the lawn. Reaching the sidewalk, he grimaced at a familiar rumble, growing louder. *I might as well get this over with.* He steeled himself.

Gideon drove around the corner. His truck slowed as he pulled up even with the boy. Sticking his head out the window, he leaned on his elbow and nailed Finn with an icy gaze. "*Never* run off again. Or else. Do ye understand?"

"Yes, sir."

"Get yer arse home. Now."

The Knight pulled into their driveway and parked while Finn jogged across the street. He followed his master through the front gate and inside.

"Now, just what was all that about? About Asher?" Gideon asked as they made their way to the kitchen.

"Nothing." Finn went to the sink and filled a glass; he gulped down half the water, stalling for time. Wiping his mouth on a sleeve, he leaned back against the counter. "Can we have lunch now?"

"Not until ye tell me what's going on in that head of yers."

"Nothing's going on."

Gideon crossed his arms over his chest and waited.

And waited.

And waited.

Finn broke.

Again.

"I just...I just...I can't stop thinking about it," he whispered through stiff lips, staring at the floor. "About what I did wrong. He died because of me." He blinked and looked away.

With a sigh, Gideon walked over to the boy. He hooked an arm around his neck and pulled Finn close to his side.

"Now, ye listen to me, boyo. Asher was killed by the enemy. Not by anything ye did or failed to do." He leaned closer, his head almost touching Finn's. "Nor by any thoughts ye had about him."

Finn sniffed and wiped his nose with the back of a hand. Swallowing a lump, he asked the toes of his shoes. "Really?"

"Truly."

Finding himself leaning against his master, part of him cringed. *He's going to think I'm such a wimp.* But he couldn't make himself pull away. They stood like that for a few minutes until Finn's stomach growled. They both chuckled.

"I best feed ye lunch before I'm accused of child abuse." Gideon let go and aimed a playful cuff at his apprentice. He smiled when Finn dodged out of the way.

With the afternoon sun throwing his shadow out before him, Finn marched across the street and back up the Steel's walk, a look of determination on his face. He squared his shoulders and rang the doorbell.

"Hi, Savannah," he said as the girl answered the door. "Can I talk to Rafe, please?"

She smiled at him. "He's in the family room." As she waved him inside, she pointed to his neck. "Hey, where's your what-do-you-call-it?"

"My torc? Oh, I...I gave it to someone."

Before she could ask another question, he hurried toward the back of the house. Hesitating in the doorway, he fidgeted until Rafe looked up from the television.

"Hey, Rafe? Look, I'm sorry I was being...you know. This morning." He curled his toes inside his shoes as he waited.

His friend punched the mute button and unfolded himself from the recliner. "Being a jerk?"

Finn nodded.

Walking over, Rafe swatted him in the stomach with the back of his hand. He grinned when Finn failed to block it. "Yeah, me, too."

Finn took a deep breath. "Something happened. While you were gone." He cleared his throat. "Um...Asher died suddenly. On the Fourth. From a stroke. We had the funeral the day afterwards."

"Oh." Rafe blinked with surprise. "So, are you okay?"

Finn nodded. *I will be*, he thought to himself.

The Journal of Finnegan MacCullen: July 9
<u>What I Learned ~~Today~~ Two Days Ago:</u>

First: Sometimes, bad things happen. And it's really nobody's fault.

Second: A friend is someone who likes you when you don't like yourself.

The Journal of Gideon Lir: July 9

Ye, gods, another attack. I scarcely reached Finn in time. He is struggling so with Asher's death; I should have checked him for a weapon before we left the house.

With the eclipse tomorrow, the Amandán are becoming bolder. What do they know that we don't know?

Mac Roth is spending hours in research, trying to bury his grief as he searches for any more clues as to the Spear's location and identity.

If we cannot find a way to stop the enemy, I fear that the Tuatha De Danaan will truly become no more than a legend.

Twenty-Eight

"Up, boyo."

Finn jerked awake as a hand nudged his shoulder. Rolling over, he stared at the silhouette of his master looming over him in the dark. The hoarse screeching of crows echoed off the walls from the open bedroom window. He sat up, his stomach doing cartwheels.

"Get dressed," Gideon ordered. "Quick, now." Without another word, he bolted from the room.

Finn flung his clothes on, his fingers clumsy as he scrambled to tie his shoes. He strapped on the ankle sheath, then raced down the stairs. Swinging around the post, he sprinted into the living room. A single pool of light spilled from the lamp on Gideon's desk.

"Here." The Knight tossed him a knife. He waited until Finn caught it, then tossed him a second one. "One on yer leg and one in yer belt."

"Is it an attack?" He bent over to slide the blade into place. "Like the other night?"

Gideon selected a dagger. He ran a thumb along its edge, then replaced it and chose a knife instead. "I'm afraid it's worse. Come."

He led the way to the darkened kitchen. "Look." He pointed out the window over the sink.

Finn stared across the back yard. Several massive dark shapes bobbed up and down on the far side of the wall. Amandán. "What are they doing?"

"Piling pine boughs along the top."

"Why?"

"Remember what I told ye—contact with bronze burns them. They'll be able to scale the wall safely once they have a thick enough layer to protect them. Now, Mac Roth is already on his way, but I'll need to hold them off until he arrives. Ye're the reserve in case something goes awry."

"We."

"Sorry, what?"

"*We'll* need to hold them off," Finn said. "No way are you going out there by yourself. I'm going with you, not hanging out in the kitchen."

Gideon lifted an eyebrow. "Oh, ye are, are ye?"

"Yes, sir." To Finn's astonishment, his master gave a nod.

"Why, then the poor beasties haven't a chance." Gideon glanced sideways, eyes aglow with the joy of battle. "Here's what we'll do."

The back door crashed open as two figures leaped out, chanting in unison. Side by side, they raced across the lawn, weapons gleaming in the light of Gideon's moonstone.

As the first Amandán clambered on top of the wall, a knife impaled the beast between the eyes. Its screech split the night.

"And MacCullen is on the scoreboard first," Finn crowed, snatching the weapon from the pile of ash. He grinned up at his master. "Did you see that strike? Now, that was skill. Bam—I nailed it right in the head."

"'Twas the luck of the Irish, nothing more," Gideon retorted. At that moment, a second goblin jumped up on the wall. Gideon slashed at its ankles and sent it tumbling toward him. Jumping to one side, he speared it in midair. The Amandán exploded. "Now *that* was skill." He pointed at the mound of gray powder with the toe of a boot. His head jerked around when Finn shouted.

"Gideon! Watch out!" Dropping a shoulder, Finn plowed into his master. He sent him staggering to one side just as a third Amandán lunged over the wall. Its fingers missed the Knight's face by less than an inch.

With a grunt, Finn stabbed upward; the cloud of ash caught him in the face. "Oh, man, right in the eyes." He wiped his face, smearing the powder even more.

Gideon reached up with a free hand and started pulling the branches toward him. Finn joined him. The tangy scent from the fresh evergreens mingled with the reek of goblin residue.

"It kind of smells like pine cleaner, mixed with a used cat litter box," Finn noted as he cleared off the wall. "Or, maybe more like turpentine poured over a baby's diaper after the baby—" He winced when a pine bough abruptly slapped him on the head, silencing his observations.

"Sorry," Gideon said, without a trace of remorse. "The bleedin' thing slipped from me hand." He tossed the last branch into the pile littering the foot of the wall. "There, that should slow them down. They'll have to fetch more from the woods."

Weapons at the ready, master and apprentice marched back and forth beside the wall. Both smiled grimly at the frustrated snarls coming from the ravine. Vegetation snapped and crunched as heavy bodies moved away through the underbrush. Stillness followed.

"'Tis peculiar," Gideon murmured, after a few minutes. He twirled the blade in his hand as he scanned the woods.

"What's peculiar?"

"They have now attacked *our* home. Twice."

"Because they think you have the Spear?"

"Perhaps." Gideon shrugged. "We'll find out tomorrow, eh?" He brightened at the distant rumble of Mac Roth's Jeep. "Ah, the cavalry approaches."

"*Heavy* cavalry," Finn muttered under his breath.

As they listened, Mac Roth pulled up with a crunch of gravel, killing the engine as he coasted into the driveway. They could hear thunderous footsteps running along the side of the house, followed by the sight of the enormous Knight rounding the corner. He held a knife in one hand and a hatchet in the other. He slowed as he spotted them lingering by the back wall.

"I hope ye left some for me." Mac Roth sauntered toward them.

"'Tis not me fault ye took yer sweet time getting here. Finn and I finished off three of them out of sheer boredom."

"Ye were always a stingy one, Lir." Mac Roth winked at Finn, leaned over the wall, and listened for a moment. "Well, maybe I'll have the luck and they'll return. I'd hate to have shown up here just for nothing."

Turning to Finn, Mac Roth laid his hand on the boy's shoulder. "And I owe ye an apology. I've not had time to speak with ye properly since Asher's funeral." Finn stiffened at the mention of the dead apprentice; Mac Roth squeezed gently. "'Tis all right, boyo. We can and should speak of the fallen. It helps heal the grief." He smiled and let go. "Thank ye for yer gift to him."

Finn nodded. "He deserved it."

Mac Roth sighed. "Aye, that he did, lad; that he did." Casting aside his sorrow, the Knight stepped closer to the wall and straightened to his full height. He threw back his head. "Beware, ye beasties," he roared into the gloomy woods. "Mac Roth of the Hundred Battles is here. And I am in a foul mood, for having to rise at such an ungracious hour to deal with the likes of ye. *Eireann go braugh!*"

The neighbor's back door creaked open. An elderly woman's quavery voice called from the adjoining yard. "Mr. Lir, is something wrong? I heard some yowling and shouting."

"Why, no, Mrs. Martinez," Gideon called back, shushing Mac Roth with a gesture. "I'm simply...um...shooing a pesky tomcat from me yard. I apologize for the noise."

"Well, all right, then." A moment later, the door shut with a click. All three De Danaan looked at each other and shook their heads.

"How come, in all the adventure stories, the hero never has to deal with nosy neighbors, doing chores, paying bills, or anything like that?" Finn asked.

"Because, Finnegan MacCullen, young warrior of the Tuatha De Danaan—" Mac Roth paused as he sighted along the edge of his knife for any nicks "—this is reality, not fantasy."

Yawning until his jaw cracked, Finn stretched, then knuckled his eyes with both hands. Sitting cross-legged on top of the picnic table, he leaned back and gazed up at the stars overhead. *It's been over two hours and nothing's happened. I wish they would just attack and get it over with.* He yawned again. Seeing Gideon glance in his direction, he snapped his mouth shut and tried to look alert.

"I saw that," Gideon called from the far corner, where he waited with Mac Roth. "Why don't ye go in now? We'll stand watch the rest of the night."

"Nah, I'm good." Finn unfolded himself and hopped down. Hobbling a few steps, he walked around the yard, warming up his legs as he listened to the Knights murmuring to each other. At the sound of his own name, he ambled closer, trying to act nonchalant as he eavesdropped.

"But I cannot understand why Finn and I have been the target of so many attacks. Just take tonight, for example. What is drawing the Amandán to *us*?" Gideon rolled his shoulders, weariness showing in the movement. "Could it be related to the Spear? Or is it something else?"

Mac Roth scratched at his beard, then smoothed his fingers through it. "Maybe I overlooked something in me research."

"Or perhaps Iona isn't telling us everything. Ye know how she enjoys playing her games."

"Only when she knows it will aggravate ye, old friend." Mac Roth glanced around and noticed Finn nearby. "Sharp ears, Lir."

Gideon pointed toward the house. "Bed. Now," he ordered in a tone Finn recognized.

"Hey, I think I'll go to bed, now." Finn spun around and headed toward the back door. As he made his way upstairs, he thought about his master's words.

What's the deal with Iona? I wonder if she really does know where the Spear is. Man, I hope we have it. Then, we can wipe out the Amandán. Once and for all.

Reaching his room, he peeled off his filthy clothes and tossed them into the corner. He crawled into bed and clasped his hands behind his head as he lay staring up at the ceiling. The cool night breeze flowed into his room from the open window.

I'm glad Mac Roth isn't mad at me, and that he doesn't think it's my fault about what happened to Asher. That he really believes it was the Amandán that killed him, not me.

He smiled in the dark as a soft voice called up to him from the backyard.

"*Codladh sumh*, Finn."

Twenty-Nine

"Ye gods." Mac Roth looked up from the kitchen table, a forkful of scrambled eggs suspended in front of him. "Gideon, there's a red-combed rooster loose in yer house."

Finn stood in the doorway, bleary-eyed as he looked around. "A rooster? Where?" He tugged up his sweatpants as he padded, barefooted, across the room and joined the Knight at breakfast, one side of his face still creased from sleep. At Mac Roth's gesture, he reached up and felt his hair sticking out furiously from his head. "Oh. Right."

Gideon stepped over to the stove and poured more eggs into the skillet with a pleasant sizzle. He glanced over. "I thought ye would have slept later. After all that happened last night."

Yawning, Finn scratched under an arm. "I tried, but I smelled bacon." He snagged a piece from the platter in the center of the table and crunched it down in two bites. "What time does the eclipse start?" He swallowed and raced Mac Roth for the last strip, snatching it out from under the Knight's paw. He stuffed it in his mouth with a triumphant laugh.

"Mid-morning—about nine-forty or so. The actual eclipse should last around six minutes." Gideon scraped more eggs onto Mac Roth's plate, then piled the rest on Finn's. After setting the skillet back on the stove, he poured himself a mug of tea and joined the others.

"Will it really go dark?" Finn asked. "Like at night?"

"No, 'tis only a partial eclipse," Mac Roth said. "The moon's too far out in its orbit to completely block the sun."

Finn crammed half a slice of buttered toast into his mouth. "So what's the plan?" he asked in a spray of crumbs. Catching Gideon's expression, he hastily wiped his lips.

"Lay out every blade in the back yard, so we can observe them all without missing anything." Gideon looked up at the clock, and chugged the rest of his tea. "We best get started."

An hour later, Finn nudged open the screen door with his toe, an assortment of knives and daggers in his arms. "Okay, that's the last of them." Carrying them to one side of the practice dummy, he placed them with the others on the ground, then stepped back. He studied the various knives, daggers, and even a few hatchets scattered on the grass. "None of them look special, so I really hope this works."

"Aye, as do we all." Gideon arranged the weapons in a circle.

Finn squinted up at the morning sun, careful not to look directly at it. "I can't tell if it's started or not."

"Very soon." Gideon checked his watch, then the sky. "Finn, go stand opposite of Mac Roth. And if ye see anything out of ordinary, anything at all, then sing out."

Finn took a position, his eyes wide as his gaze darted around and around the circle. While he watched, shadows began to gray as the moon slipped between the earth and sun. The unnatural fading of light and color sent a chill up Finn's spine.

I can see why ancient people freaked out during this, and made up all sorts of rituals to bring the sun back. It's creepy to me, and I know what's going on. Pressure began to build in his lungs.

The Knights jumped at Finn's sharp intake of breath.

"Sorry," he said, sheepishly. "I forgot to breathe."

Mac Roth muttered something about feeble-minded apprentices, while Gideon shook his head and resumed the vigil. His eyes moved from blade to blade, face expectant. Blushing, Finn looked down, hoping to be the first to find the Spear. Several more minutes passed.

The sky grew lighter. Shadows deepened and colors glowed as the moon rolled away. Birds chirped from the tree in the corner. A breeze from the woods brought the scent of warm pine. The Knights raised their heads and stared at each other, sharing a look of dismay.

"Ye gods, Gideon. It's not here."

"Perhaps *'the dark sun'* means something else."

"Could Iona have been wrong? Or, could we have missed something?" Mac Roth tugged at his beard. "I think I'll ring her up, right now." Before Gideon could protest, Mac Roth hurried inside. After several long minutes, he returned, scratching his head.

"Well?" Gideon and Finn asked, at the same time.

"She says she has recently discovered more information about the Spear, but she'll only speak to us in person."

"Us?" Gideon knitted his brows in suspicion.

"As in, ye and me. She said that if ye truly desire her help, ye are going to have to come to her."

The Knight clenched his jaw. "Is there no other way?" He growled in frustration when Mac Roth shook his head. "Once again, we have to play her chess game of life and death."

"'Tis the only way, me friend." Mac Roth hesitated for a moment, then continued in an undertone. "I know ye believe she had a hand in what happened with—"

Gideon's eyes flashed blue ice. "Not *believe*. I *know* she did." He tried another tactic. "One of us needs to stay and observe. The Spear may yet reveal itself."

"Let me stay," Finn interjected. "I'll watch, while you go talk with Iona."

"Are ye daft? Leave ye alone here, after what happened last night?" Gideon shook his head. "Not bleedin' likely."

"Actually, the boy has a point," Mac Roth said. "We only need one pair of eyes here. And he's safe enough, now that we know the Amandán's little trick. Anyway, yer house is secure against attack, so he can always take refuge inside."

Gideon studied Finn. "Promise me ye'll go directly inside if they come back? No heroic attempts to fight them off?"

"I promise," Finn said. A thrill shot through him. *The Spear might still do its thing, and I'll be the one to find it. Then I'll be a legend, too!* His scalp tingled at the thought. Schooling his face, he added solemnly, "I won't do anything stupid."

The Knights were still laughing two minutes later, as they pulled out of the driveway and drove away.

Finn picked at a scab on his elbow until it peeled loose. He flicked it away. Leaning back on his hands, he sat on the grass and stared at the circle of blades. A glimmer of amber caught his eye. Scrambling to his hands and knees, he crawled closer, his gaze never leaving the simple knife. Holding his breath, he leaned closer.

"Rats. Just a reflection." Settling back down, he crossed his legs and plucked a stem of grass. After folding it lengthwise, he held it to his lips and blew gently, trying to make it whistle. *Got to get Rafe to show me that trick again.*

The thump of running feet and faint voices echoed from the other side of the ravine. As he jumped up, they began to fade. *I bet that's Rafe and Savannah. I thought they ran with Mr. Steel earlier in the morning.*

Hurrying over to the wall, he hoisted himself on top and stood. The bronze-clad rocks were slick beneath his feet. As he watched, two figures raced away from him, along the trail winding through the trees and up into the hills, the smaller one in the lead. They disappeared over the top of the ridge. *Savannah is* so *going to make the cross country team,* he thought. *I wonder what it's like to go to school. All day. Every day.*

With a *swoosh* of wings, the first crow flew past.

Finn jerked his head up. His shoes slipped from beneath him on the smooth metal. Flailing his arms, he tumbled into the yard, landing awkwardly on one knee. More birds passed overhead. Their caws split the morning on their way to the foothills. Following his friends. His heart flip-flopped as he remembered the Amandán's words during the attack at the lumberyard.

We'll hunt yer mates down, soon enough. Give them a taste of what happens to humans who join up with ye De Danaan.

Finn tore his eyes off the crows. He stared down at the ring of bronze weapons, their tips all pointing toward the center. Thoughts ricocheted back and forth inside his skull.

Rafe and Savannah are out there. What if the goblins go after them? They don't know how to fight. Rafe will try to save his sister, but the monsters will grab them. Just like Asher. They'll grab them and then...and then...

But what about the Spear? He doesn't say it, but I know Gideon thinks the Amandán are going to finally finish us off. That we are doomed as a people.

"Ye gods, what am I supposed to do?" he whispered. "Go, or stay here?"

Finn hesitated, his gut twisting. Then, he tightened his lips and grabbed two knives from the circle. As he knelt down to slip one into his ankle sheath, he froze and stared at the gap left by the two missing weapons.

The gap helped form a new shape; an unfinished circle with open ends.

Like a torc.

Finn ran. He tore uphill, along the trail, with a knife clenched in one hand, gasping a line from the Song. "'I am a wind on the sea'." His legs burned as he shot over the crest. Catching his wind on the downhill, he sucked in a deep breath and shouted Rafe's name, his voice echoing through the silent forest. He slowed to listen.

No answer.

Picking up speed, he turned a corner and followed the trail as it ran parallel to the slope. He hurtled along, banked around another curve, and plowed up the next hill. Reaching a three-way fork in the trail, he skidded to a stop, his chest heaving. *Oh, crap. Which way?* Cupping his hands around his mouth, he hollered again, swerving side to side. "Rafe! Rafe, where are you?"

Savannah's scream ripped through the woods.

Finn whirled toward the sound. Stumbling over a root, he fell to the ground with a grunt. The gravel tore his hands and knees, while the knife sailed into the underbrush. He lurched to his feet and dove in, cursing as he pawed through the vegetation. Locating the weapon, he gripped the handle, ignoring the pain of his bleeding palms. A red trickle ran down one wrist.

Savannah cried out again, her voice rising in anger.

He took off, running north. Ahead of him, an outcropping of rock appeared, towering over the tops of the nearby trees. He knew what lay at the cliff's feet.

The place where Asher had died.

Finn sprinted the final yards. With a shout, he hurtled through the bushes surrounding the clearing.

Thirty

Savannah shook Rafe's restraining hand off her arm. "Stay behind me," she yelled, swinging a branch as the monster from a nightmare crouched a few feet away.

"Yeah, right." He crowded next to her, trying to grab the stick from her hand. "And give me that."

"No way. Get your own," she gritted through her teeth, taking another swipe.

With a stroke of its paw, the Amandán smacked the branch out of Savannah's hand. It spun away and landed by the foot of the rock wall.

"*Nar*, if it isn't the De Danaan's little friends," the creature rasped in delight. "Ever since that whelp killed two of me mates, I've been wanting to meet ye."

"Oh my gosh, it *talks*," Savannah breathed.

Rafe raised his chin. "What do you want with us?"

The Amandán licked its lips. "Why, to invite ye to supper." A twisted grin split its muzzle, the smell from its yellow mouth sour as vinegar. Spreading its massive arms wide as if to embrace its prey, it lowered its head and charged.

At that moment, a figure leaped into the clearing.

"Shut your eyes!" Finn landed between the goblin and his friends. With a grunt, he buried his blade in the beast. He ducked his own head as the Amandán exploded, ash blowing everywhere. The knife fell to the ground with a clatter.

Finn snatched up the blade and scanned the area. "Are there more?" he panted. At the silence behind him, he glanced over his shoulder. "Guys! I said, did you see any others?"

They both flinched at Finn's harsh tone. "N-no," Rafe said. He stared at the pile of ash by his feet.

Edging back toward them, Finn kept the knife at the ready as his eyes swept the surrounding woods. "Listen, we've got to get out of here and back to my house. We'll be safe there."

"What are those things?" Savannah asked. Her face and clothes, like her brother's, were dusted with a coating of grayish powder.

"I'll explain everything when we—" He froze. A shadow flitted across the clearing. Narrowing his eyes, he watched as the crow circled overhead. "This is not good."

"More of those monsters?" Savannah asked.

Finn nodded. Turning around, he looked at his friends. *They're going to think I'm crazy no matter what I tell them, so I might as well tell them the truth.*

"They're called Amandán. And, yeah, they're real. Whatever you do, do *not* let them touch your head or face with their hands, or you'll die. From a stroke."

"Can we fight them?" Rafe fingered the bracelet encircling his wrist.

"Heck with that." Savannah stooped to tighten the laces on her athletic shoes. "Can we outrun them?" Glancing at her brother's confused expression, she added. "Hey, I may be brave, but I'm not stupid."

Finn pulled at his pant leg and slid the second knife free. "Here." He passed it, handle-first, to Rafe. "Bronze destroys them." He gestured toward the pile of ash with his own blade.

"How do I...?" Rafe held the weapon tentatively as he looked at Finn.

"You stick them with the sharp end." He watched the crow as it continued to wheel in the sky above them. *Do we try to make a run for it? Or do we stay and keep the rock to our backs? Either way, we're screwed.* He glanced at the Steels, trying to decide. *Maybe I should ask them. It's their lives, too.*

"So here are our options—run like heck, and hope we don't stumble into any other Amandán that are out there. Or stay here, and fight them off. This cliff is defensible and they can't sneak up behind us."

The Steels looked at each other.

"Run like heck," Savannah said.

"Stay and fight," Rafe decided.

All three stiffened at the sound of movement in the nearby bushes. Twigs snapped. Behind a thick stand of scrub oak, a dark form rose. It swayed from side to side, then vanished. The forest held its breath.

Before the boys could stop her, Savannah scurried over to the rock wall and snatched up the fallen branch. Gripping her weapon in both hands, she pushed her hair out of her face and took a stance between them.

"Keep your backs against the cliff," Finn instructed. "And hold tight to your weapons—it's easy to lose them during a fight." His eyes flew back and forth, trying to watch all sides at once. He wiped his still-bleeding palms on his tee shirt, then took a firmer grip on the blade. "Here it comes!"

The Amandán burst from the underbrush. Knocking Savannah off her feet with its shoulder, it dodged under Finn's swing and lunged at Rafe. Gritting his teeth, Rafe stabbed and missed. The goblin hissed and slapped at the boy's arm. The weapon flew out of his hand.

"Watch out!" Finn jumped in front of his friend just as Rafe dove for the knife. They crashed into each other, the impact sending them both to the ground. Finn groaned in dismay as his own knife disappeared into the nearby bushes. Rolling to his feet, he grabbed Rafe and shoved him over next to his sister. Weaponless, he turned to face his foe.

I'm going to die here. And so are Rafe and Savannah. The realization tore through him as the Amandán snarled and popped its knuckles, preparing for the kill. Then it charged.

In desperation, Finn grabbed the goblin's wrists, frantic to keep its scrabbling fingers away from his head. Its ugly mug filled his vision; he was sure he could see up the goblin's nostrils and right into its skull. Tightening his grip, he struggled to keep his feet under him as the Amandán flung itself from side to side.

"Let go, ye little tick," it snarled.

All of a sudden, the Amandán froze. Then, with a piercing shriek, it yanked loose, howling in agony as it swiped at its wrists where Finn had touched them. Foam began spewing from its mouth like soda from a shaken can. Convulsing spasmodically, it collapsed, face hitting the ground. Its hands and feet clawed at the dirt. With a final jerk of its limbs, it shuddered to a halt.

It lay there in a stinking heap.

His chest heaving, Finn stared down at the dead Amandán, an odd humming in his ears. He blinked. Black dots began dancing in the corner of his vision. He shook his head, blinking again. Lifting his hand to rub his eyes, his arm felt heavy, as if the bones had turned to stone. Swaying, he stuck out an unsteady leg and poked the carcass with his toe, gingerly at first, then harder.

"How did you do that?" Savannah asked as they approached, grimacing at the carcass. "Phew! Do they always smell this bad?"

Finn nodded once, his mind reeling. He watched as Rafe picked up the other knife.

"I think we should pull a Savannah, now," Rafe said.

"What's that?" his sister asked, the cudgel back in her hand.

"You know. Run like heck."

Something heavy and fast thundered through the woods; more than one pair of feet pounded against the ground, charging toward them. Perched overhead on the clifftop above them, the crow gave a final caw and flew off over the treetops.

The three looked at each other, their faces streaked with sweat and goblin residue. Turning to confront the approaching enemy, they stood shoulder to shoulder. The crashing and splintering sound swelled, as if the monsters were determined to tear down every tree to reach them. Trembling from more than just nerves and fear, Finn sucked in a shaky breath. The humming in his ears rose to a high pitch as the world dimmed around him.

Suddenly, a call rang through the hills like a battle horn. His heart leaped at the familiar voice shouting the ancient war cry.

Gideon burst into the clearing a moment later, Mac Roth on his heels. The Knights skidded to a halt when they spotted the dead Amandán. As Finn watched through mounting darkness, his master lowered his weapon and started toward him. He could see the Knight's lips moving, as if shouting something, but there was no sound. Finn swayed, desperate to stay upright.

Then, the ground rushed up to meet him.

Thirty-One

Gideon caught Finn in his arms just before his apprentice hit the dirt. Ignoring the slurred voice complaining about being picked up, he carried him over to the edge of the clearing. Dropping to one knee, the Knight lowered him onto a clean patch of grass. "Are ye with us, boyo?" He patted the boy's cheek.

Finn blinked. "W-what happened?"

"Ye passed out. Or very nearly." Gideon eased him upright into a sitting position.

"Whoa. Talk about a head rush."

After a few minutes, Finn gave a nod, took Gideon's proffered hand, and pulled himself to his feet. He looked past the others hovering nearby and gazed in wonder at the dead Amandán. "Did I really do that?"

"Aye." Gideon blew out a long breath. "Ye gods, Finnegan, ye found it. Ye found the Spear."

Finn shook his head. "It wasn't the Spear. I...I grabbed the Amandán, and it spazzed out, and then it just *died*."

"What?"

As Finn explained, Mac Roth flipped the carcass face-up with his boot. "'Tis certainly well and truly dead." He squatted down and ran the tip of his knife through the foam coating the beast's lips. "It looks like it's been poisoned." He stood up and exchanged glances with Gideon.

"Ye said ye simply seized it, and then it died?" Gideon asked Finn. When Finn nodded, he looked over at Mac Roth. "Are ye..." he began.

"...thinking what I'm thinking?" Mac Roth finished.

"Aye, I am. Finn, let me see yer hands." As the apprentice held them out, Gideon reached over and ran a finger through one of the seeping wounds. "Yer hands were bloodied *before* ye touched it?"

Finn nodded again. "So, how come it didn't turn into a pile of powder afterwards?"

His brows knitted in thought, Gideon reached into his back pocket and pulled out his handkerchief. Using his knife, he sliced the fabric in half and began bandaging Finn's wounds.

"Gideon?" prompted Finn.

A corner of the Knight's mouth twitched as he worked. "Could it be that simple, Mac Roth? It seems so far-fetched."

"Maybe this is what Iona meant, when she suggested we think about it from a more symbolic angle," Mac Roth replied. He began ticking off his fingers. "A deadly weapon that can kill an Amandán outright. One that is in yer possession. And 'twas created by a De Danaan and a mortal. In a matter of speaking."

"Perhaps." Gideon thought for a moment. "But I would rather she not know about all this, just yet."

"Distrustful of her still, are ye?"

"Always. Me instincts tell me to wait before we inform her. Agreed?"

"All right, Lir," Mac Roth said, reluctantly. "For now."

"Uh, what are you guys talking about?" Finn winced when the master pulled the cloth tight and knotted it.

"Put the clues together, boyo."

"The clues to what?"

"To the identity of Gideon's Spear, ye thickheaded apprentice." Gideon rapped his knuckles against Finn's skull with an affectionate *thunk.*

"But I told you, I don't have the Spear." Finn rubbed his head.

The Knight rolled his eyes as Mac Roth tried to smother his laughter in his beard. Finn's face reddened in indignation. Before the boy could protest, Gideon placed both hands on his shoulders and gave him an affectionate shake.

"Finnegan MacCullen. Are ye not half mortal, half Tuatha De Danaan?"

"Well, yeah, but—"

"And are ye not *my* apprentice?"

"Yeah, but—"

"And did ye not *destroy* that Amandán with yer bare hands, *covered in yer blood?*"

"I guess. But what does that have to do with…" Finn froze in mid-sentence. His eyes and mouth formed perfect O's.

"And the light dawns."

"*I-I-I'm* Gideon's Spear?" Finn's voice cracked as he stammered. "But…but I'm a halfer."

"No, you're a Tuatha De Danaan. In every sense of the word." Gideon smiled at his apprentice. "We'll speak more about this later. For now…" He turned to Rafe and Savannah. "I'm not sure how to explain to ye who and what we are." He added, after a moment, "Nor to yer parents."

"Finn told us a little," Rafe said. "But maybe you should start at the beginning."

Finn laughed. "It's a long story."

"It's a long walk back," Savannah pointed out, still holding her club. She took a position between Finn and Rafe as they followed Mac Roth single-file down the path, the giant already expounding on the history of the Tuatha De Danaan. Gideon fell in behind them, on the heels of his apprentice.

As they made their way through the woods, he noticed Finn wincing as he tried to hold his knife, first in one injured hand, then the other. "Put yer weapon away, boyo." As Finn paused to slip it into the ankle sheath, Gideon added. "I'll guard yer back."

Thirty-Two

Finn spun the basketball in his hands as he slouched on a beanbag in the corner of Rafe's bedroom. He tried to balance it on the tip of a finger, then gave up. Making a face, he tossed it over to Savannah, sitting cross-legged on the bed.

"Do you think you made the right decision?" he asked Rafe, who was working at his desk. A twinge of envy snaked through Finn as he stared at his friend's laptop, but he pushed the feeling aside. "Not telling your parents about what happened yesterday?"

"I do," Rafe said, scrolling through his e-mail. "I mean, we're fine, and Mr. Lir made sure we got home okay, so no harm, no foul. And anyway, I can see me trying to explain to Mom and Dad about these monsters that wanted to chow down on Savannah and me. Or that we were saved by our neighbors, who happen to be these not-really-human-but-close-enough magical Irish warriors." He snorted. "Yeah, I don't think so."

"Are you still going to ask your grandfather about Padraic O'Brien? See if he's a De Danaan, too?" Finn looked over just in time to catch Savannah's return toss of the basketball.

"Yeah, as soon as I can figure out a way to do it without sounding crazy."

"Good luck with that." Finn sent the ball back to Savannah. "I better get home. Gideon and I are going out hunting again this evening, when he gets back from the farmer's market."

"Farmer's market?" Rafe asked.

"Yeah, potatoes are a lot cheaper there." Finn sighed. "And we eat a lot of them." He rolled to his feet and started for the door. He glanced back at the sound of Savannah's voice.

"Hey, Finn?" She grinned, her dimples deepening. "Thanks again. For what you did for us."

A tingle shot through his stomach at her smile. He blushed when Rafe made a gagging sound. Without a word, he smiled back and left.

Still wearing a loopy grin, Finn ambled home. *I've got to figure out how to protect them,* he thought. *Since they've become prey, too. It'd be a lot easier if their parents knew, but I'm not sure they could handle the truth about us De Danaan. At least, not yet.*

He began humming, breaking into song after a few steps. "*Fire in the head—I'm a flame in motion,*" he sang. "*Fire in the head—I'm a sword that's sharp. Fire in the head—I'm a drop in the ocean, a shield in battle and a string in a harp.*"

Halfway across the street, his voice died away. He slowed and squinted into the late afternoon sun. A sedan was parked in front of their house and there was no sign of Gideon's truck in the driveway. As he reached the other side, the driver's door opened. A young woman in a navy suit, her brown hair pulled back in a clip, climbed out. A file folder was tucked under one arm.

"Hello. Are you Finnegan MacCullen?"

"Yeah." Finn edged around the car and took a stance by the front gate. "Who are you?"

"I'm Ms. Ubarri, from the Department of Human Services." She walked closer, halting a few feet away from Finn. An identification badge dangled from her lapel. She glanced at the empty driveway. "May I ask you a few questions?" Her eyes traveled over his face and bare arms as if looking for something. She seemed disappointed.

Warning bells began ringing in Finn's ears at the title of the department. "About what?"

Plucking a pen from her pocket, she opened the folder and wrote in it. "About you. And your guardian…" she paused to check a sheet "…Gideon Lir. Am I pronouncing it correctly?"

"Close enough." Finn moved closer to the gate and twined his fingers through the wrought iron.

"I understand you've lived here since late May. Is that right? And that Mr. Lir is an old family friend of your aunt and uncle?"

The bells clanged louder. "How do you know all that?"

Ms. Ubarri's eyes flicked across the street toward the Steels' house. Pushing back a stray strand of hair, she tapped the folder with her pen. "Oh, it's all here in your records." She pasted an earnest expression on her face. "Now, before we begin, I want you to know that *anything* you care to share with me will be kept private. I promise."

"You mean private from Gideon?"

"Well, yes."

"I'm not supposed to keep secrets from him."

She made another note. "Do you think he might become angry if he knew you had talked with me, Finnegan?"

"I go by Finn, not Finnegan."

"All right. Finn it is. So, does he get angry often?"

"What do you mean?"

"Well, when you do something wrong or misbehave, does he yell at you or..." She waited, letting the unspoken words hang in the air.

Finn tightened his lips and said nothing. Her questions about his master raised the hackles on the back of his neck. *I know what she's hinting at. She thinks he knocks me around.* Shifting to one side, he glanced down the street, willing his master's truck to appear.

Ms. Ubarri softened her voice. "You seem nervous. Are you afraid he might do more than scold you? Perhaps hurt you in some way, if you…" She paused at the low rumble of an engine drawing closer.

Finn looked past her. Relief flooded him when the gray truck appeared at the far end of the street and rolled toward them. As Gideon pulled into the driveway, he brushed past Ms. Ubarri. Hurrying to the vehicle, he reached it as his master climbed out of the cab with a squeal of rusty hinges.

"And just who might that be?" Gideon kept one eye on the woman, as he reached into the truck bed for a knobby burlap sack.

"Some lady from the Department of Services for Humans, or something like that."

The Knight's face darkened. "What does she want?"

"She said she wants to talk to me about *you* and that she knew all about me and it would be a private conversation and then she asked me if I was afraid of you and if you would hurt me…" The words spilled out of Finn's mouth faster than his tongue could keep up. He gulped a breath when Gideon patted his shoulder.

"Easy, boyo. I'll take care of this. Wait here." Flinging the dusty bag of spuds over one shoulder, he walked toward Ms. Ubarri.

Finn hoisted himself up onto the wall of the truck bed. He drummed a heel against the side, then stopped, trying to listen. His master and the woman spoke for several minutes, the Knight shaking his head with every other sentence. Their voices grew louder. In frustration, Gideon flung the bag down in a puff of dust. Ms. Ubarri stepped hastily back, in fear for her polished shoes.

"Sir, I will not divulge who contacted us," she snapped in a carrying tone. "But since—"

"'Twas Steel, wasn't it?"

"—but since a report of possible child abuse has been made," she continued in a cold tone, "this file will stay active until proven otherwise, or until the person reporting it drops their accusation. And you should know, there may be future visits from our department."

Gideon's mouth worked, but before he could speak, the woman spun on her heel and left, her car pulling away from the curb with a jerk. Finn hopped down and jogged over. Side by side, they watched the sedan turn the corner and disappear.

"Well, boyo, we've got another issue to deal with, thanks to bleedin' Rufus Steel."

"What do you mean?"

"Do ye recall all the times he asked ye about the cuts and bruises ye acquired whilst training or hunting with me?"

"Yes, sir."

"Well, I'll bet me torc he thought *I* was the cause, and he reported me. So, now I am under suspicion." He blew out a long breath. "I know the man means well, but now we're going to have to be doubly chary about ye getting injured."

"I'll be more careful. I promise." Finn picked up the sack at their feet. He followed Gideon through the gate and into their home. After dumping it on the kitchen counter, he went back into the living room.

The Knight handed him a knife. He waved aside his master's offer of a second weapon and patted his lower leg. "I'm packing one already."

"Good lad." Gideon selected a knife for himself. Sliding it into the sheath, he studied Finn for a long minute. "I must admit, I'm still concerned about yer faintness after ye grappled with the beastie."

"Do you think it has something to do with me being, um, the Spear?" He blushed as he said the words aloud for the first time. *I don't know if I even want to be that. I just want to be a Knight. Like Gideon.*

"I do."

Finn shook his head. "It just all seems so weird. I mean, I don't *feel* any different. I still feel like me."

"Ye gods, what a relief. I was just about to take a knee, and bow me head in reverence to yer newly acquired magnificence."

"Really?"

"No, of course not, ye dolt." He chuckled at Finn's huff of exasperation. "Finnegan MacCullen, the Spear of the Tuatha De Danaan ye may be, but ye're still an apprentice with a great deal to learn. And not just about hunting Amandán."

"Aye, 'tis true," Finn replied, in a passable imitation.

Gideon laughed, the lines of his face softening. "By the way, I've something for ye." He took a seat at his desk and tapped a finger on a thick packet sitting in front of him. Colorful stamps littered a corner of it.

"What's that?"

He waved Finn over, gesturing toward the stool. As he sat down, the Knight leaned back in his chair, his face carefully neutral. "It arrived for ye today, in the post. I believe Mac Roth may have had something to do with it."

Finn picked it up and paused to peer at the stamps, fingering the package. "The Republic of Ireland? I don't know anyone there." He tore it open. A bubble-wrapped, flattish object slid onto the desk. Picking it up, he peeled off the plastic; his eyes widened at the first hint of gold. As the final layer fell away, his heart swelled, pushing at an odd lump in his throat.

"Oh," he breathed. His face glowed as he gazed down at the object.

The new torc gleamed in his hands.

keep reading for a sneak peek of:

Gideon's Spear

Book Two
of
The Adventures of
Finn MacCullen

One

Screamingly bored out of his mind, Finn blew out a long sigh as he wandered around the clearing in the woods. The last rays of the summer sun lit the trees surrounding him, coloring the trunks of the Ponderosa pines with a shade of bronze that matched the large knife, almost the length of his forearm, held in one hand. With a snap of his wrist, he flipped it into the air and caught it by the handle.

Holding the weapon level with his eyes, he tilted it to and fro, trying to view his reflection in it. For just a moment, he caught a flash of blue eyes in a boyish face dusted with freckles, and a mop of hair the same flaming color as the blade. Adjusting the angle downward, he grinned as he was further rewarded with a glimpse of a twisted rope of gold, as thick as the Knight Mac Roth's thumb, encircling his throat just above the collar of his tee shirt. "You are, Finnegan MacCullen," he murmured to himself while adjusting the torc so that the twin knobs on the ends of the neckpiece were dead center under his Adam's apple, "a total badass warrior."

Gravel crunched behind him.

He whirled around. "Oh, crap." His heart rammed against the roof of his mouth at the sight of his worst nightmare.

His master, the Knight, Gideon Lir.

Pissed off.

Again.

The black-haired man, dressed in a denim shirt and work boots, stomped down the path toward him, slashing at the undergrowth on either side with an enormous hunting knife when it dared to impede him. To Finn, he seemed to grow twice as large with every step.

"What the bleedin' 'ell are ye doing?" Gideon began yelling while still a few yards away.

As if he wants the entire state of Colorado to hear him, Finn thought. *Which he probably does.*

"I ordered ye to stand safe by that tree, not mince about admiring yer beauty."

"I'm sorry, Gideon. I was just—" The rest of his sentence was cut off when his master grabbed him by the arm and hustled him backward, pushing him none too gently against the massive trunk.

The Knight's eyes, the same uncanny blue as his apprentice's, narrowed when he reached out and tapped the torc around Finn's neck. "And if *this* is distracting ye from our evening's hunt, then we should just be rid of it. I know of an abandoned gold mine not three miles from here I could pitch the thing into." He held out an open hand.

Finn reached up and clutched the torc protectively. "Ah, come on, Gideon. I've only had it for a few days. Look, I'm totally focused now." He shifted his wiry body into battle stance, legs shoulder-width apart and weapon held across his body at the ready. "Just show me one of those ugly goblins and I'll—"

They both froze when a shape alighted on the ground next to them in a clap of ebony wings. Muttering to itself, the crow strutted closer. It reached out and pecked at Finn's athletic shoes as if trying to untie them.

"Steady, boyo," Gideon whispered.

"I hate these things," Finn muttered back, curling his toes inside of his shoes. The crow cawed as if laughing at him.

"Aye, but they're bleedin' useful. When they're not playing us for fools." As the bird aimed another peck, Gideon stomped a boot at it. "*Whist!* Flee unless ye've something to warn us about, ye black devil."

The crow hopped back with a squawk of indignation, then spread its wings and hoisted itself into the air. They watched as it made a loop over the trees tops. A second bird joined it. Both crows whirled around each other in anticipation before soaring away, taking the last rays of sun with them.

Master and apprentice's heads whipped around when a branch snapped a few yards up the trail.

Gesturing for Finn to stay put, Gideon eased across the clearing and along the path on silent feet. Paying close attention to the deepening shadows, his eyes swept the area. He tilted his head, a wolf on the hunt, as he listened to the rustles and scratches of the twilight.

As Finn watched, exhilaration and dread wrestled with each other inside of him as they always did when he and his master were hunting the Amandán.

Or being hunted by them.

A figure burst out of the bushes. With a growl, a creature, not quite human, not quite ape, launched itself at the Knight. Its black-tipped fingers scrabbled for Gideon's face.

Twisting to one side, Gideon dodged as the Amandán hurtled past him. He stuck out a foot. A yelp spilt the evening when the goblin tripped, then hit the ground and tumbled end over end into the undergrowth. Scrambling to its feet and red-eyed with rage, it charged the Knight again, running slightly sideways on all four, its dark green pelt blending in with the vegetation. "*Poc sídhe,*" it hissed through yellow teeth. Dirt and twigs spewed up behind its feet as it came.

"*Poc sidhe* yerself." Gideon shifted his grip on his knife and made a *come along* motion with his hand. The goblin sped up. Just as the Amandán leaped for him, he dropped to one knee. Chanting a line from the Song under his breath, he buried the weapon in the goblin.

With a shriek, the Amandán exploded into a cloud of grey-green ash. Gideon ducked his head, trying to shield his face from the worst of the powdery remains. He waited until the cloud drifted away with the evening breeze before rising. "*Bah.*" He spat to one side. Wiping his mouth, he strolled back to Finn waiting by the pine. "Amandán taste as disgusting as they smell."

Finn nodded. "Kind of like burnt rubber." He took his master's blade when Gideon handed it to him to hold.

He watched as the Knight peeled off his shirt, gave it a brisk shake, and draped it over a tree limb. A Celtic knot, tattooed on his master's right arm, peeked out from under the sleeve of his tee shirt. Finn stared at the tattoo, the ancient symbol of Knighthood amongst their people, the Tuatha De Danaan. *Ye gods, I'll never be as good at hunting or fighting as he is. Of course, if he would let me do* more *hunting and* less *drills, I might get better at it.*

Gideon cleaned the blade on his jeans. "Now, since the beasties often hunt in pairs, we'll see if we can't catch the second one before it goes to ground."

"Can I circle around and flush it out?" Finn asked, shifting from foot to foot.

The Knight hesitated, then shook his head. "I'd rather ye not track that far ahead of me."

"Why?"

"Because it's too dangerous."

"Ah, come on, Gideon, I want to—"

"I said no."

"But, how can I learn anything if all I do is follow you around?"

Gideon's face darkened. "Arguing with me, boyo, is as dangerous as hunting the Amandán."

"But I've fought them before." Finn's voice cracked in frustration. "I know—"

"Ye know less than ye think. A few skirmishes with the goblins do not make ye ready to hunt alone."

"Why won't you let me at least *try?*"

"Because ye're not ready!"

Finn scowled. "It's because of the whole Spear thing, isn't it?"

"Oh, aye, that's it," Gideon said, heavy on the sarcasm. "Discovering me apprentice of less than two months is none other than the legendary Spear of the Tuatha De Danaan has made me decide to treat ye differently from now on."

"It has?" Finn's heart sank. *I'm sick of always being different. I just want to be a Knight. Like Gideon and Mac Roth and all the other De Danaan.*

"No, ye dolt." Gideon reached out and cuffed him lightly on the side of the head. "I don't care if ye're the High King on the throne of Tara, ye'll continue to learn the ancient ways of the Tuatha De Danaan. To meet our enemies in battle, armed with knife and dagger and the strength of our Song."

Finn nodded. An odd relief filled him. "Okay. I mean, yes, sir." He blinked in surprise when the Knight laid a hand on his shoulder and gave it a squeeze.

"Remember, boyo. Gideon's Spear ye may be. But ye're also Gideon's apprentice." He sighed dramatically. "More's the pity for me."

Finn grinned. "Ah, me heart bleeds for ye now, to be sure," he said in a pitiful imitation of the Knight's Irish lilt. He ducked and came up laughing when his master swung another cuff at him and missed.

Failing to hide a smile, Gideon turned and led the way up the path. Stepping around the pile of ash in the middle of the trail, they continued westward, climbing deeper into the foothills through the growing dusk. Around them in the woods, squirrels rustled about in the dried leaves under the scrub oak bushes, hiding caches of acorns. A breeze began flowing down from the mountains further west, cooling them as they walked along.

The shadows around them thickened. After a mile, the Knight paused long enough to dig into his jeans pocket. He pulled out a small white stone, its edges translucent. Almost immediately, it began to glow in his hand, illuminating the woods around them with a pale light. He held the moonstone aloft and scanned the area. Up ahead, to one side of the trail, a pair of enormous boulders leaned against each other to form a cave about the height and width of a man. Or an Amandán.

Standing behind his master, Finn gasped when the moonstone's beam caught a pair of greenish eyes, like a cat's, in the cave's opening. "Um...Gideon," he whispered.

"Aye, I see it." Raising the stone higher, he called out. "Come along, beastie. I've something for ye."

"*Nar*, I know what ya gots for me," the Amandán growled back. "I seen what ya did to me friend back there." It spat. "No, I'll just stay in here. Out of reach of that nasty piece of bronze ye be carrying." It made a smacking sound with its lips. "Unless ya want to send that whelp of yers in here after me."

"What, and waste a perfectly good source of free labor? Not bleedin' likely." He spoke over his shoulder. "Finn, I want ye to move around to the side while I..."

"Did ye say *Finn?*" the Amandán said. Its eyes disappeared briefly as it turned its head and hooted into the interior of the cave. Signaling. "Ye be the Knight, Gideon Lir." It hooted again, louder this time. "We hears some wild tales about ye and that whelp there."

Voices echoed from within the cave. Finn looked down in confusion when the gravel by his feet began bouncing about like Mexican jumping beans. Tremors vibrated through the soles of his shoes. The vibrations grew stronger, mixed with harsh cries and shouts.

Next to him, Gideon stiffened. "Ye gods," he cursed under his breath, then spun around and shoved Finn back down the trail. "Flee!"

Finn ran for his life. With Gideon on his heels, he tore down the path, feet finding their own way over rocks and roots. Bushes and boulders and black-barked trees flashed past in the dusk. Turning his knife hilt-first as Gideon had drilled into him, he gripped it tight as he sprinted along.

"Faster, boyo," the Knight shouted behind him. "And don't stop until ye're safe home."

Too busy concentrating on not tripping to answer, Finn dug deeper. Panting, he began chanting a line from the Song, singing the swiftness he needed. "I am a wind on the sea."

A tingling began somewhere around his ankles, then coiled up his legs, picking up speed until it seemed to burst out of the tips of his hair. His ears thundered with the roar of the wind, whether from the Song or from his pace he wasn't sure. He kept chanting as he shot along the trail.

Breathing in rhythm with his pounding feet, he followed the trail eastward. Ahead of him, the lights of High Springs winked through the trees. As he neared their neighborhood, he yelled over a shoulder. "Do you think they'll chase us right to our backyard?" When Gideon didn't answer, he slowed and risked a peek back.

The trail was empty.

Skidding to a halt, he whirled around, gulping for air as he stared into the darkness. His eyes darted from side to side as he strained to catch a glimpse of his master. Off in the distance, a pale light flickered once, skipping off the treetops, then vanished.

Finn hesitated. He glanced back at the line of backyard fences dividing the suburban neighborhood from the woods. Their own house, tucked away by itself on the end of the street, was marked from the desk lamp he had left on in his second-floor bedroom. His master's voice echoed in his head as he stared at the square of light.

Always leave a lamp burning for ye when ye hunt, boyo. 'Tis a signal to other De Danaan, just in case.

In case of what, Gideon?

In case ye do not return.

Rubbing the back of his hand across dry lips, Finn turned his face westward. *I know he told me to go home. But there's no way I'm leaving him to face all those Amandán by himself. And knock it off*—he ordered his trembling leg muscles. Wiping sweaty hands on his jeans, his palm brushed against the lump in his pocket. He reached in and pulled out his own moonstone. Cupping it in his hand, he looked down at it. *Wish it would light up for me like it does for pure-blooded De Danaan—I sure could use it right now.* "Being a halfer sucks," he muttered to himself. Shoving it back into his jeans, he clutched his blade and started back up the trail.

Face streaked with goblin residue and sweat, Gideon lifted his moonstone higher, its light flashing red along the blade of his knife. Mounds of ash overlapped each other on the ground between the Knight and the remaining goblins. He eased back against a rocky outcropping and bared his teeth, his eyes glowing battle blue.

"Come along, ye manky beasts. Me blade is growing cold."

"*Nar,*" one of the goblins snarled back. "It be yer bones growing cold when we be through with ye." It licked its lips in anticipation.

"Too bad yer whelp turned tail and ran," spoke another one. "I likes me De Danaan young and fresh."

"I just likes mine dead," a deep voice growled. "The day will come when ye high and mighty—" it stopped to spit out the name "—*Tuatha De Danaan* will be nothing but a pile of leftovers. And Eire will be ours once more."

"*Ach,* not the auld grievance again," Gideon said, tedium in his tone. "Ye think the death of all De Danaan will return the green isle to the likes of ye?" He raised his chin. "Ireland will never be yers again. Danu gave it to *us* to hold."

"We hads it first," the first goblin hissed. "We be the true heirs of Eire. Us the Bog-born, not the feeble offspring of some upstart goddess."

Gideon curled his lip. "Yet here ye are. In Colorado. *Not* Ireland."

"We could says the same thing about ye De Danaan—"

"*Bah,*" the second Amandán interrupted. "Too much talking, not enough killing. Let's get him, mates." The pack closed ranks.

Bracing himself, Gideon began singing the first lines of the Song, lifting his voice to rise above their grunts. As the first goblin cracked its knuckles in preparation, he dug his feet into the earth. Keeping one eye on the pack, he shoved the moonstone back into his pocket. In the sudden darkness, his knife gleamed dimly in the light of the early stars. He raised the weapon in defiance. "And who would like to be the next to die?"

The pack swarmed him.

Leg muscles burning, Finn gritted his teeth against the stitch in his side as he sprinted up another hill toward the sound of battle. Growls of rage mingled with shrieks of agony. The fear of being too late whipped him along.

Coming to a junction in the trail, he slowed to a rubbery-legged jog. After a few steps, he stopped and listened, trying to hear over his wheezing breath. A shout yanked him northward; he took off at a dead run.

He crested the next hill. Ahead of him, dark shapes milled back and forth at the foot of an outcropping of rock. Howls of laughter filled the night as they closed in for the kill.

Out of breath and out of time, Finn skidded to a halt a few feet away. He raised his knife.

And slashed it across the palm of his left hand.

"Son of a goat!" White-hot pain punched him in the gut. Before he lost his nerve, he switched hands, his blood making the leather grip slippery. He cursed when he dropped the knife; snatching it up, he drew the blade across his right palm. Hissing from the pain, he tossed the knife to one side and threw himself into the fray.

Slapping his right hand on the back of the hindmost goblin, he waited a moment, in agony that his strategy wouldn't work. When the beast threw back its head and screamed, froth spewing from its mouth, Finn lunged for the next one. A quick swipe of his left hand and another goblin died in a convulsive fit.

When a third Amandán crashed to the ground at his feet a second later, Finn staggered a step. A wave of dizziness washed over him. The sounds of the battle faded as a humming began in his ears; his bones felt concrete-heavy. Shaking his head, he swallowed, trying to focus. He dug his nails into the wounds, sucked a deep breath, then yelled as loud as he could.

"*Faugh a ballagh!*" A tiny corner of his mind rolled its eyes when his voice broke.

The remaining Amandán jumped. They whirled around at the boyish voice screaming the dreaded war cry. Tripping over each other to face this new threat, they forgot about the Knight now behind them.

Fatal mistake.

The rearmost goblin exploded with a shriek as Gideon sank his blade between its shoulder blades. Charging through the cloud of ash, he lowered his shoulder and plowed into the next two, knocking them off their feet. A quick strike right and then left, and two more vaporized.

Caught between anvil and hammer, the Amandán panicked. They tore off up the trail. Some of them bypassed the path and crashed through the underbrush. One hesitated and looked back at the dead goblins sprawled near Finn's feet. It curled its lips before following the pack into the woods.

The last wisps of left-over goblin drifted away on the night breeze, leaving a stench in its wake. In the distance, the snapping and breaking of branches faded as the Amandán fled back to their cave. Blinking against the growing wooziness, Finn search around until he located his knife; bending over and picking it up took all his strength. Gravel crunched nearby. He looked up.

"And just what are ye doing here?" Gideon walked toward him, swiping his weapon on his jeans with quick, vicious swipes. "I ordered ye home."

A dozen excuses crowded Finn's mind. For some reason, the lamest one came out. "I...I turned around. And you weren't there. So I came back." He found it harder and harder to focus. He blinked again. Without warning, his legs folded beneath him.

Author Notes

I began the rough draft of this book in the spring of 2010 after hearing about the fairy rings of southern Africa from my sister, Kelly Austin, who journeys to that most ancient of continents every year. The fairy rings led me to revisit Celtic mythology, which in turn, led me to the Tuatha De Danaan and the story cycle of *Fionn mac Cumhail*. Twisting those stories and mythologies around until they were rooted in our modern world, I came up with Finnegan's (sorry, I mean Finn's) first adventures.

However, *Finn Finnegan* had to wait another year and a half while I concentrated on my Griffin series. But once the second book in that series was launched, I returned to Finn MacCullen and discovered he was now demanding that *his* story be told.

For those readers who want to know more about the roots of my book, herein lies a brief lesson:

Finnegan MacCullen: My protagonist is based loosely on the Irish legend of Finn McCool, or Fionn mac Cumhail. This story cycle, called *The Boyhood Deeds of Fionn mac Cumhail*, follows the adventures of Finn as he grows from boy to legendary warrior.

Lir: The warrior-father from *The Children of Lir* story cycle. All I really took from that cycle was the name Lir. However, Gideon's name is a nod to the legendary Welsh figure *Gwydion*. That character was a warrior, but also a bit of a trickster. I took that trait and gave Gideon a sarcastic bent.

Mac Roth: A friend and strong right arm to one of the early kings of Ireland. A fitting name for Gideon's old friend and avuncular figure to Finn.

Warp spasm: This, too is a part of Celtic lore. This battle frenzy gave warriors extra strength and speed, and helped them ignore injuries until after the conflict.

Torc: A neck ring made from strands of metal twisted together. Most were open-ended at the front and were worn as a sign of nobility and high social status. Many examples of these have been found in European Bronze Age graves and burial sites.

Deadnettle: A plant used as a curative tea amongst various peoples in northern Europe and the British isles.

Amandán: Mythical Irish and Scottish figures which are said to reside in fairy mounds. They are feared because it is believed their touch (called the fairy stroke or *poc sidhe*) is said to causes paralysis or death.

The Song of the Tuatha De Danaan: The words that open the novel and are recited by Finn in Chapter Four and throughout the book are a portion of the famous early Irish "Song of Amergin." This translation is from the article "Echoes of Antiquity in the Early Irish 'Song of Amergin'" by Lloyd D. Graham, 2010.

Fire in the Head, a modern version of "The Song of the Tuatha De Danaan," lyrics by Arthur Hinds, performed by Emerald Rose (www.emeraldrose.com), is quoted in Chapter Thirty-Two.

Gideon's favorite song, **The Minstrel Boy**, was written by Thomas Moore; 1779-1852.

Fairy (fey) rings: Round, barren patches of soil are found throughout Namibia, South Africa, and Angola. These circles are devoid of vegetation and range from several feet to several yards across. According the Himba people of southern Africa, these circles are said to have been created by gods or spirits.

You and I know better.

Acknowledgements

It has been said books are not created in isolation, and an author is only as good as her editor. Aye, 'tis true. I have been blessed with two extraordinary warriors of the word craft: Vikki Ciaffone and Trisha Wooldridge. Thanks and thanks and evermore thanks to this amazing duo. Trish, for sticking a dagger down the back of her pants to see if a weapon can be carried that way. (The answer is: no, not really.) And Vikki, for the phrase "write your geek." It has become my motto for life. Both of them have wicked senses of humor, and I spent most of my editing time howling with laughter. Which the best way to edit. Laughing, not howling.

I will also take a knee in gratitude to my publisher, Kate Kaynak, who believed in the Celtic magic of *Finn Finnegan* right from the start. She, and the entire team at Spencer Hill Press, is a shining example of just how good a publishing company can be. *Gle mhaith* to you all.

And, as always, to Wes. Thank you for being my Knight.

A portion of the net profit of each copy of *Finn Finnegan* goes to **The Topnaar Education Fund** to help provide education to the children of the Topnaar people of Namibia, Africa.

The Topnaar Education Fund (The Gava Kids) is a non-profit organization focused on providing education for selected students from the Topnaar people in and around Walvis Bay, Namibia. They work with leadership from within the Topnaar community to identify children based on need; most are either orphans or are from extremely compromised family situations. For more information, visit them at: www.gavakids.com

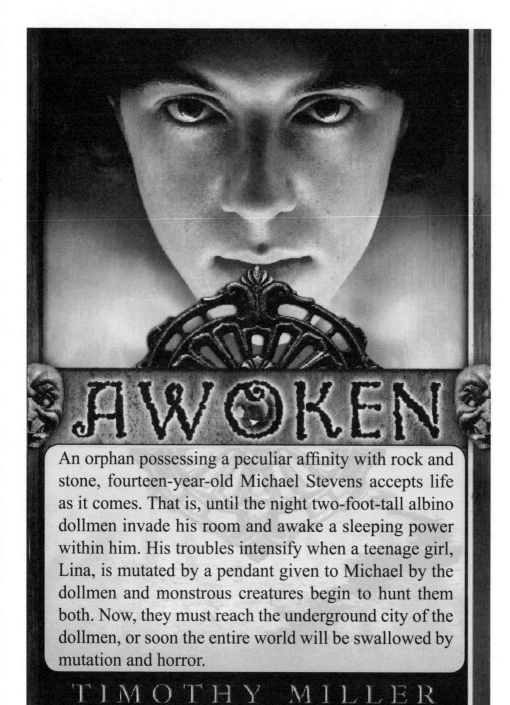

AWOKEN

An orphan possessing a peculiar affinity with rock and stone, fourteen-year-old Michael Stevens accepts life as it comes. That is, until the night two-foot-tall albino dollmen invade his room and awake a sleeping power within him. His troubles intensify when a teenage girl, Lina, is mutated by a pendant given to Michael by the dollmen and monstrous creatures begin to hunt them both. Now, they must reach the underground city of the dollmen, or soon the entire world will be swallowed by mutation and horror.

TIMOTHY MILLER

AUGUST 13th 2013

Also available as an ebook • SPENCER HILL PRESS • spencerhillpress.com

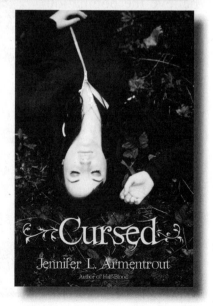

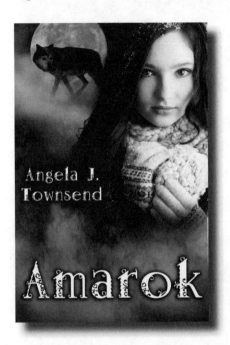

THE LOST IMPERIALS · BOOK ONE

SHERRY D. FICKLIN & TYLER H. JOLLEY

EXTRACTED

An infamous brother and sister have been stolen from history and drafted to opposite sides of a war no one can win—a battle for time itself.

Founded and run by the disembodied head of a mad genius, the Tesla Institute is responsible for locating, retrieving, and training teens with the ability to Rift through time and space. Seventeen-year-old Ember has no memory of her life before being brought to the Institute, but she's made a home there. Just as she's about to officially join the ranks of the Rifters, memories of her bloody past begin to slide through the cracks. Now she's forced to question everyone she loves and everything she's been taught.

Ex still bears the scars from the fire that killed his entire family. The newest member of a group of rogue Rifters known as The Hollows, he thinks he's finally found his place in the world. It's gritty and treacherous and the only place he feels completely free. But his partner and best friend Steinward is dead, and he's to blame. The only chance of saving her is a dangerous mission inside the heart of the Tesla Institute itself. But what he finds there is more than a piece of tech. It's the key to changing his whole life. Now that he understands what's possible, he's willing to break all the rules to put his family back together.

Also available as an ebook • **SPENCER HILL PRESS** • spencerhillpress.com

About the Author

Award-winning author Darby Karchut has long been fascinated by mythologies and hero stories from around the world. She attended the University of New Mexico, graduating with a degree in anthropology. After moving to Colorado, she then earned a master's in education and became a social studies teacher.

Drawing from her extensive knowledge of world cultures, she blends ancient myths with modern urban life to write stories that relate to young teens today.

She currently lives in Colorado Springs, Colorado, with her husband, where she still teaches at a local junior high school. She enjoys running, biking, and skiing the Rocky Mountains in all types of weather, and owns more backpacks than purses. As she should.

Finn Finnegan is the first in *The Adventures of Finn MacCullen* series. Her other young teen books include *Griffin Rising* and *Griffin's Fire* (both from Twilight Times Books).

Visit her at: www.darbykarchut.com